Michelle Cleaster

Before The Fall

Kim Williams

Michelle Cleaster
Before The Fall

Sa'Quon DeEse Publishing
Lahaina, Hi.

visit www.saquondeese.com
for additional information and special content.

Printed in the United States of America

Dedicated to my Grandma

End of the school year Essay
Contents

End of the year Essay

SECTION #1

Essay INTRODUCTION:

Yesterday I saved a world, and today at school it didn't even matter. That's the reality of middle school, it's like everything is opposite, backwards and turned upside down. All that really matters is how popular you are. And if you're not popular nothing you do really matters. I don't fit in, it's like I'm from another planet or something... either that or everybody else is.

Don't get me wrong, I'm not a total looser, I do have some skills. To the world outside of school I am a twelve year old crime fighter, genius inventor and daughter of the most celebrated investigative mind on the planet, but at school I'm just the six foot tall freak.

Let me back up. My name is Michelle Cleaster and to be honest, my mouth does tend to get me into trouble and I've been known to have a little bit of an attitude and maybe I do exaggerate... sometimes. Oh yeah, my best friend Bella says I might have a split personality.

(Hey... are you talking about me? Sure sounded like it...)

But she is only joking... I think. Besides, Bella is a too tall freak like me, but she acts like she isn't.

(Can you say denial?)

Both of our dads are tall enough to play in the NBA. Bella says we get our height from them, it's genetics so there is nothing we can do about it. She tells me I shouldn't care what the other kids think and she's right of course. But no matter how hard I try not to, I do.

Anyways, this essay is an assignment for school. Each year as the school year comes to a close, the school puts together a time capsule. I am supposed to document the world of 2030 as I see it, so enough about me.

Chapter 1

A LASER BLAST tore right through the overturned table I was hiding behind and exploded a huge wad of gum someone had stuck to the underside. Slimy, melted chewing gum went everywhere.

(Now that's just nasty.)

I was in an old abandoned restaurant or something... I wasn't sure. Whatever it was, I was running out of places to hide.

Two more blasts tore almost identical holes in the table and came within inches of my nose.

(That was close, too close...)

I was on the case of the missing middle school basketball team and had stumbled into an ambush. I glanced around the room and spotted the kidnappers hiding behind the bar. There was a five gallon bottle of some nasty looking liquid on a shelf just behind them. I fired a laser blast into it, showering them with smelly, slimy goo and then I watched them scatter.

(Yeah, that freaked them out.)

"Bella, where are you," I shouted into my radio.

"I'm almost done, I cut a hole in the back wall. I can see them, but everyone is tied up, so I will have to untie them before I can get them out... I need more time," Bella replied, "You've got to keep distracting them."

"OK, but make it fast, their aim is improving."

I peeked around the table again; I could see the little weasels running around. I eased away from the overturned table, crawling on my belly across the foul smelling carpet.

(Really?! ... This carpet reeks.)

I ducked behind another table before shouting out a question.

"Honestly, who in their right mind kidnaps an entire basketball team?" The distraction worked, the sound of my voice coming from a different part of the room surprised them and they responded with a volley of poorly aimed laser blasts that only managed to set a nearby chair on fire.

Someone shouted, "We did it because nobody pays us any attention. Every game it's the same thing, no one even thinks about us until they want something. We figured if there was no basketball team then we would get more attention!"

(Wait a minute, I recognize that voice. That sounds like the kid who works at the 'Snack-Shack', the skinny pimply faced kid with the hooked nose... what was his name... Jeff!)

"Jeff, is that you?"

"Uhhh, No," Jeff lied.

"Jeff, Dude... Buy a clue."

"How do you know my name?"

"You sold me a hotdog at the game last week!"

"Oh... well... that wasn't me. I mean, this isn't Jeff."

"Yeah it is, Jeff c'mon... people come to see the basketball team play. Nobody comes to see you and your friends sell hotdogs at the snack shack!"

Jeff popped his head up and shouted, "we don't care and we won't let them go until our demands are met." Another laser blast ripped through the cabinet above my head. I ducked instinctively and rolled behind the vending machine.

Sparks were flying from laser blasts that were shredding the vending machine. I had to dive onto the floor and I was starting to get annoyed. It wasn't so much getting shot at with laser pistols.

(...*by the zit king who works in the snack shack.*)

What bothered me most was the carpet really, really stunk and no matter how hard I tried, I kept landing on it... it was making me gag.

"How about a compromise," I said while ducking behind another overturned table. "How about we let you perform at halftime, during the halftime show and we'll get someone else to sell the hotdogs while you're away."

"No! We want it all," Jeff said, "and we won't let the team go until you do what we want."

(*Well, that didn't work, anymore bright ideas?*)

I had to move each time I spoke so they couldn't follow my voice and surround me. I fished out a smoke bomb from my back pack and tossed it towards the sound of their voices, then used the thick smoke to hide my movements.

"Smoke bombs, are you kidding me, I thought you were supposed to be tough," Jeff shouted.

I managed to get behind Jeff and his evil gang of snack-shack servers and hid behind a booth.

Jeff poked his head up and said, "Really, a smoke bomb, is that the best you can do. Come on out and fight you coward,"

"Or we could talk a little more and try to work this thing out," I shouted back.

Jeff and his lame snack shack gang were startled; they spun around and started shooting wildly into the area of my voice.

(*Or not.*)

I prayed silently for an answer and then an idea popped into my head.

"We all have a role," I said calmly, "we need each other if this thing is going to work. An eye can't say to a foot that it's not needed. Each part is important, nothing is indispensable. Working at the snack shack is important stuff."

"Don't you try to confuse us with that Christian stuff," Jeff yelled, "we are angry and we're not listening."

I was thinking about my next move when Bella's voice came over the radio.

"Michelle, I got em all... I already called the FBI, they should be arriving any minute. We're on our way back to the school."

"Fantastic, I'll meet you there," I replied and then I addressed the 'snack-shack pack'.

"Hey guys, I just have one more thing to say".

Jeff shouted, "Nothin you say will change our minds!"

"OK, how bout this... we rescued the hostages and the FBI has you surrounded."

"Ha Ha Ha, that's two things dummy... wait a minute... Nooooooooo!" The kidnappers screamed as the FBI moved in to take them into custody.

(He made terrible hotdogs anyway.)

Before long I was in my nuclear powered flying car on my way to pick up Bella.

As I lifted off I couldn't help but think about what had just happened. Then for some reason my mind drifted to the abundance of Reality TV. There were so many these days. Reality TV game shows had replaced everything... even sports. People could communicate via text-messages and twitter and vote on what they wanted to see the contestants do. And the contestants wanted to be on TV so bad, whatever got the most votes... they did it.

(It's amazing what people are willing to do just to get a little attention. Romans 2:8 warns of wrath and fury for those who are self-seeking. I think we all could stand a little self examination instead.)

***

I landed in the Huber Middle School parking lot. The parents were hysterically hugging their rescued children when I entered the cafeteria where the reunion was taking place. I was uncomfortable being anywhere inside this school. It was an almost visceral reaction that is difficult to explain. It's like waking up inside a port-a-potty and discovering there were no doors.

(I have to get out of here.)

I spotted Bella, my best friend and trusted sidekick as she drifted towards the refreshment table. There were cookies and punch and other goodies spread out on the small table to celebrate the Basketball Team's rescue. I made eye contact with Bella and signaled for her to come over. I knew Bella didn't particularly like to be interrupted when she was about to consume massive amounts of empty calories and it showed in her expression when she walked over.

***

"What's up?" Bella asked when she got within earshot; her mouth was stuffed with cookies.

"We have a new emergency, let's roll," I said.

"But they haven't even cut the cake yet."

"Stop thinking with your stomach."

Bella sighed and said, "you need to pace yourself. At this rate there won't be any bad guys left and then what are you going to do?"

I didn't respond, but I did cross my arms and roll my eyes.

"I'm just sayin..."

I tapped my foot and raised one eyebrow the way our teacher Mrs. Esposito does when someone is trying her patience and said, "Are you coming or not?"

Bella shoved another cookie into her mouth and looked longingly back at the uncut cake before she said, "Oh alright, but don't say I didn't warn you."

***

SECTION #2

Essay BODY:

The world in the year 2030 is very different from what everyone imagined back in 2010 when my parents met and married. A lot of small countries got together and combined to make super countries. Like, all of South America is now one huge "continental country" and so on and so on.

Over the last twenty years America has gone through some drastic changes too. The United States of America has merged with Canada and Mexico and Central America to form the United States of North America.

The second "Industrial Revolution" came and went and the only thing we have to show for it is a gigantic toxic cloud of thick brown smog. It's about the size of Australia and it roams freely around the globe. It has become a force of nature like a hurricane, so they gave it a name... "Jessica".

"Jessica" is so toxic that whenever she's in the area, alarms sound. Fearful men would cower in shelters while women snatched their children off the streets.

***

Chapter 2

AS SOON AS Bella and I stepped out of the cafeteria the "Smog Alert" sirens began to wail. They reminded me of the "Air Raid" sirens in the old war movies. The "Smog Alert" sirens only went off when "Jessica" was coming. Most of the time "Jessica" stayed high up in the sky, but occasionally it would drop to ground level.

(The air in Los Angeles was bad enough...
but one breath of "Jessica" could kill you.)

These days everyone carried gas masks for such an occurrence. We both pulled out our gas masks and put them on before sprinting to the car. Every car had powerful filters as standard equipment, so the car should offer us some protection.

"Ok... what's the emergency?" Bella asked when we were seated in the car and safe from "Jessica".

"The 'Emergency' is that I can't stand being there!"

Bella groaned. We lifted off and banked hard to avoid the approaching toxic cloud.

"Well, I'm hungry," Bella said.

I sighed and shook my head.

"What? A girl has to eat. Besides," Bella pointed out, "now that 'Jessica' is in town, there won't be power for long."

"OK I guess we could go home, I'll make us each a vegetable smoothie."

Bella made the universal sign for gagging by sticking her finger in her throat. Then she looked out the window and spotted a fast food restaurant below.

"How about a McKinley's Colossal burger?"

Mckinley's was a relatively new but fast growing chain of fast food restaurants that sprang up when the government severely relaxed regulations. By law they were not permitted to call their meat "beef", and though everyone now knew what it "was not" ... there was no law in place that required them to say exactly what it "was" either.

"I thought we agreed no junk food on a school night!"

"With 'Jessica' in the neighborhood, I doubt there will be school tomorrow. So technically this isn't a school night," Bella said with a grin.

"Whatever," I said as I began landing procedures.

***

"Hello Rita," I heard Bella greet the girl at the register, apparently after reading her name tag. "Two Colossal Burger meals, please."

I was busy putting away my gas mask. When I glanced up and saw both Bella and Rita looking at me expectantly, I knew something was up... then it hit me.

"Why do I always have to pay?"

"What? I would pay except I left my wallet in the car," Bella lied.

After I reluctantly paid for the meals, Rita left and returned with a plastic tray that had two mystery meat patties, each with a slice of cheese on top.

"What's this?" Bella asked looking down at the tray.

"It's your meal."

"No... It's two meat patties and cheese, where's the rest of it?"

Rita sighed and pointed at the sign on the counter, it read:

Due to the short supply of vegetables, anything made from vegetables will be temporarily unavailable.

The management

"That means if you want a bun, which is made from wheat, you hafta come back another time when they are available. If you want ketchup, pickles or onions, which are..."

"I know what pickles and onions are," Bella said cutting Rita off.

"No fries?" I asked.

"Fries are made from potatoes and..."

"Never mind..." Bella said picking up the tray.

"I don't make the rules, I just work here," Rita complained. Next she reached under the counter and pulled out a small metal can. She shook out two tokens and dropped them on the tray. Bella glared at the tokens and then back up at Rita.

"The tokens are for the water machine," Rita said answering Bella's unasked question.

"For the record," Bella said just before she turned from the counter, "ketchup is made from tomatoes and tomatoes are fruit and wheat is not a vegetable either it's a grain."

Rita didn't say anything, but she did stick her tongue out.

***

SECTION #3

Even a trip to a fast food restaurant can be an adventure these days. You never really know what you are going to get depending on supplies and stuff. For example, in the old days of self-serve soft drinks, so I've been told, you simply walked up to the soda machine and pushed the button to dispense the soda. Obtaining a soda in a restaurant these days is a two step process. The first step is to obtain the water from a coin operated water machine and then you added the syrup later.

Air and water were most essential for survival. So in addition to a gas mask, everyone carried their own filter cup to process clean drinking water. The cup had two chambers. The top chamber collected the dirty contaminated water, filtered it and produced drinkable water into the bottom chamber.

***

Chapter 3

I **WALKED UP** to the water machine and dropped in the token. Then I watched as the light brown/green untreated liquid filled the top part of my cup, went through the filtration system and came out clean drinkable water when it dripped into the bottom half.

"That stuff sure does stink," Bella said while holding her nose. I didn't respond, I just stepped aside and handed Bella her token.

"I wonder where it comes from." Bella said, thinking out loud while she filled her cup.

"Well fresh water disappeared from the planet years ago. All water is recycled, so I will give you one guess," I said as I nodded towards the bathroom.

"Yuck, that's disgusting," Bella said.

"Well, you can't live without water... hey just pretend you're an astronaut that's where they got their drinking water for years."

"I almost lost my appetite."

"It's disgusting, but it's safe. Where do you think the water you drink at home comes from?"

Bella glared at me and said, "You know stuff like that, you need to keep to yourself."

I laughed and said, "Until we can solve this pollution problem it's the way things are."

It didn't take long to finish off our mystery meat patties and cheese. We washed it down with polluted punch and it was time to get back to work.

***

By the time we got back to the car there was a message from the team of scientists at the "Botanical Preserve" high in the Sierra Nevada Mountains.

"Someone stole all of the trees from the Endangered Forest section of the Botanical Preserve," I said while I punched the buttons to pull up the report on the in-dash computer for Bella to read.

"You're kidding right? Those five trees are the last trees in the entire country. Scientists are using them to repopulate the continent, who could have done such a thing?"

"I'm not sure, but I have a pretty good idea."

***

We arrived at the outskirts of the estate belonging to Rich Wellhoff after following the trail of dirt and leaves from the preserve. This was pretty easy since trees were nearly extinct there weren't any other leaves on the ground. Mr. Wellhoff made his fortune in oil. But the oil had run out years ago and the world had reluctantly switched to solar.

Unfortunately whenever "Jessica" arrived, it blotted out the sun. By midday there wasn't enough sunlight to power many of the solar devices. Which meant that it was a bad day for a getaway since Mr. Wellhoff's equipment ran out of power mid-heist.

Jessica had gained altitude so there was no longer any danger to the people on the ground. I swooped in beneath "Jessica" and spotted Mr. Wellhoff and his men below, frantically trying to cover-up the trees.

Mr. Wellhoff was an obnoxious little fat man who only considered his needs with little concern for how it affected others.

"You are going to have to return the trees Mr. Wellhoff," I said as I approached the fat man.

"What trees?"

"Uhhh the tall brown things behind you," Bella said pointing to the trees in large wooden planters.

"Those are my trees."

I said, "Trees have been nearly extinct for years."

"I don't believe it; I think the tree-huggers are making all of it up." Both Bella and I looked at him, waiting for him to laugh at his obvious joke. He didn't.

"I think he's serious," Bella said out of the corner of her mouth. "There haven't been any trees since 'Animal Planet' merged with the 'History Channel', where has he been?"

"Look around," I said, "haven't you noticed that there are no trees?"

Wellhoff looked around and said, "Well I see five trees right over there."

"Duh yeah," Bella said, "they are the last five trees in the country and you just stole them."

"I don't care, I want to build a deck for my pool and for that I need wood. And wood comes from trees. Now that I have them I am not giving them back," Wellhoff said as he signaled to his goons. "My men are here to protect me and my trees. So as you can see there is nothing you can do about it."

I sized up the goons who were beginning to surround us snarling and cracking their knuckles.

Bella said, "The police are on their way."

Wellhoff laughed and said, "Look up, there's no sun, the police don't have power. I have horses on the way to pull my trucks. These trees will be long gone before the police arrive."

"For once in your life if you ever considered doing the right thing, now is the time," I said.

Now that made Wellhoff laugh.

Bella made a show of counting his goons, "Only six? You are going to run out of goons long before we break a sweat."

The fat man laughed again and said, "You are just a couple of twelve year old girls, you can't tell me what to do." Then he turned and spoke to his biggest goon, "please escort these children away from me and my trees."

I probably should have told the fat man that Bella and I were both masters at Krav Maga, a hand-to-hand combat system used by the Israel Defense Force (IDF), FBI, Swat and the United States Special Forces. But it must have slipped my mind, besides, he was going to find out soon anyway.

It didn't take long to deal with the goons. Then I turned my attention back to the fat man.

Wellhoff looked around at all of his fallen goons and surrendered with barely a whimper.

***

The police arrived and took the fat man and his goons into custody. I watched as some of the last trees on Earth were loaded onto a truck for transportation back to the preserve.

(God originally planned for us of be stewards of this planet. I guess we didn't do a very good job.)

***

Our "Base" was in the attic of my house. My dad, with help from Bella's dad had built it. It was filled with computers and lab equipment... everything a "tween" crime fighter would ever need. Since, in their absence... Bella and I were attempting to temporarily fill their shoes and continue their work.

"OK what's next," I asked Bella when we made it back to Base. "Nothing, that's it... there are no criminals left," Bella said.

"Impossible," I scoffed, "there must be some criminals somewhere. Get on the phone and contact the FBI, have them send over their ten most wanted list, there must be a new list out by now."

"I already checked, the FBI reports 'negative' there isn't one. We captured number ten last week and there is no one left to put on the list."

"Ok then, contact the CIA perhaps we can capture some terrorists for them."

"Negative there are no terrorists left, we caught the last one last month."

I sank back into my chair and sighed, "now what am I going to do. If I go down stairs now my mom is going to make me do chores!"

Bella chuckled, "I told you to pace yourself but you wouldn't listen."

***

SECTION #4

As bad as things were pollution wise, Bella and I were taking care of business in the crime fighting department. And at least for now the world was a quiet, safe place to live. There were very few bad guys free to cause trouble, because Bella and I had captured them all. Of course there were a few bad guys that we had yet to capture. But they were in hiding while they plotted and planned future diabolical acts against humanity.

School will be out soon, summer is close. I don't have any plans yet, but I am sure I will think of something.

In the meantime, I managed to keep myself busy. I had several projects to work on after school and on weekends, not the least of which was trying to solve the global pollution problem. I also completed several new and exciting inventions including a personal teleportation device. However, I spent most of my spare time searching for my father who had disappeared on a mission several months ago.

It was the case of the mysterious man who was suspected of having a secret base beneath what is known as Salvation Mountain near the California/Mexico Border. I didn't have all of the details but I did know that my dad, along with Bella's dad, disappeared while investigating the man and the mountain. We knew if we could find the mysterious man of Salvation Mountain there was a good chance we would unravel the mystery surrounding our missing dads...but that was a story for another time because we would soon be called upon by God to save an entire planet.

Chapter 4

Three months later

WE FINISHED OUR homework and worked late into the night following up on some leads related to our fathers' disappearance. Unfortunately we came up empty. Frustration and fatigue found us and we decided to stop for the night.

I was sound asleep when the emergency phone started ringing. The emergency phone was a direct line between my house and the Oval Office. I commanded my eyes to open, but, only one obeyed. And even then it focused on the clock and not the ringing phone.

"3:00 am!" I groaned. It had been a long time since my services were needed but a small part of me wanted to go back to sleep. Inwardly I was happy to finally get some action. Outwardly, I have to admit, I wished these emergencies would pop-up at a more reasonable hour.

(Even a genius crime fighter needed her beauty sleep... didn't she?)

I looked across the room. Bella was in her bed, well at least half of her was... her butt was on the bed, her head was on the floor. She was sound asleep. She looked so peaceful, naturally I thought about waking her up.

(What? Why should I be the only one awake?)

I tried to get my body to move but nothing was cooperating. The ringing stopped and I was able to relax again.

(Must not be an emergency after all.)

My thoughts were interrupted by a soft knock on the bedroom door.

"Michelle... telephone... it's the President," my mom announced from the hallway.

"OK... got it," I shouted back at the door. I popped from beneath the quilt, rolled over and picked up the phone.

"Michelle the crime fighter here!"

"Please hold for the President," the efficient voice said.

While I waited for the President I turned on my computer and started my web browser. Next I launched "You Tube" from my bookmark bar. The "You Tube" website was almost loaded when I heard the President come on the line.

"Michelle... we need you! How soon can you come to the White House?"

"Right away, Madam President, I am at your service."

"Fabulous... it's six o'clock in the morning here in Washington D.C. The Vice President and I are just getting home from a night of... ummm... international trade negotiations and we... "

I stopped listening. The President had a habit of babbling so I developed a habit of tuning her out when she did. I "searched" the recent postings on "You Tube" for the President's name and there were already videos of the President and Vice President posted. I doubted partying at a British pub qualified as "international trade negotiations," but I decided not to press the issue and let it go.

"... can get a few hours sleep while you make the necessary arrangements to fly here from Los Angeles," I heard the President say when I tuned back in.

"Well actually," I interrupted, "I've invented a teleportation machine. It's capable of teleporting me anywhere in the world in seconds. Give me a minute to shower and get dressed, Bella, and I can be in your office in less than thirty minutes."

"That soon?" The President asked hesitantly.

"Yes ma'am, I could be there sooner except it takes a few minutes for me to get my hair under control."

"Ah man!" I heard the President mumble just before the line went dead.

(I tossed my pillow at Bella to wake her up.)

The pillow startled Bella, she fell off the bed with a loud thud, and then bounced to her feet.

"I'm alright," she said looking around... scanning the room... totally confused.

I couldn't hold it, I started cracking up. When Bella turned to look at me I could have sworn I saw steam coming out of her ears. I dodged a flying shoe as I ran for the bathroom.

(What an ingrate, at least I used a pillow to wake her up. I could've used a shoe.)

***

SECTION #5

Politics as usual, were in the headlines and our new president was really stirring things up. But I'm getting ahead of myself, let me back up a little and explain.

Eight years ago the United States of North America elected Constance Mannage their first woman president, I really liked her, she was strong and smart and she got the job done. And for the first time in a long time, America experienced relative peace and prosperity. These days the president is allowed to serve three terms as opposed to the traditional two. Unfortunately after eight years of the leadership of President Mannage, Americans had grown weary of peace and prosperity.

Years ago there were a lot of fake celebrities who were famous simply for partying and being drunk and acting stupid. As they got older a lot of them went into politics and because they were well known for being fake famous, they got elected.

So when Americans went to the polls this time they elected party girl and fake celebrity Allison K. Hollick President. Nobody thought she would do a better job, she just happened to be more popular.

(I guess America was more like middle school than

I thought. And yes, I am aware of the irony. It would seem the Ex-President and I have something in common. But I won't even go there.)

***

Chapter 5

WE MATERIALIZED IN the oval office less than twenty minutes later.

"Good morning Madam President," I said as cheerfully as possible, considering it was 3:25 AM by my internal clock. I didn't get a response from the President who was seated behind her desk with her head down on folded arms.

I looked around the oval office. The Vice President was on the presidential couch, passed out, snoring loudly. The little dog the Vice President was known to carry tucked inside a designer purse, stuck his head out and growled at me before retreating back into the purse. The dog had lost most of its hair and all of its teeth. It looked more like a large toothless rat than a dog... it was harmless.

The President was drooling all over some important looking presidential papers on her desk. Bella read the president's name plate it said "Allison K. Hollick".

"Allison K. Hollick," Bella said out loud, "Allie K. Hollick... Allie-k-Hollick... get it!"

I laughed when I ran the name through my head, then I caught myself. I tried to get the president's attention again by clearing my throat, it didn't work. But it did cause the little hairless dog to poke his head out again and bark, which caused the President to stir.

(Whatever works)

President Hollick struggled to raise her head then smiled weakly.

"Glad you could make it," she said. Then she looked at me and cocked her head like a confused puppy. "Why is everything red?"

"I think it's because your eyes are bloodshot, Madam President."

"Oh yeah, that makes sense."

"You wanted to see us about an emergency Ma'am."

"I did? Oh yeah I did." The President sat up and tried to wipe the drool from her mouth but she missed the drool and her mouth.

(Yuck!)

"That's an amazing invention, can I try it?" The President asked, suddenly coming alert.

I shook my head and said apologetically, "Unfortunately the devices only work on Bella and me... on our individual DNA... I'm sorry but it won't work for you."

"Just think of all the shopping I could get done if I had a teleporting thingy... please let me try it out just once," President Hollick gushed.

"Madam President..." I tried to get a word in but was ignored. I was starting to get frustrated so, I took off my shoe and held it up so the President could see it. I spoke slowly.

"Madam President," I said "the teleporting thingy is built into my shoe. It's tuned to my DNA. If you used it to teleport yourself, there is no guarantee you would be the same when you reached your destination. You could re-materialize as a donkey or even a bowl of jello."

Bella leaned in close so that only I could hear and mumbled, "Let her use the shoes, a donkey or a bowl of jello might be an improvement!"

I almost laughed out loud.

"Stop it Bella," I whispered out of the side of my mouth.

"I'm just sayin... "

I nudged Bella with my foot cutting her off, Bella straightened up and giggled.

Luckily the President hadn't noticed because she was still talking about shopping.

The President said, "I would be in and out... I wonder if my secret service detail would need to teleport too, they hate it when I just disappear..."

The Vice President stirred on the couch.

"... I suppose I will have to get their shoe sizes and then..." the President continued to babble.

I tried to think of a way to get her attention without being rude. As if on cue the Vice President rolled over and fell off the couch. Next the Vice President climbed back onto the couch with a confused look on her face. Her hairless dog poked his head out and started barking. The Vice President stood, stretched, scratched her butt and then sat down on the couch still dazed and confused.

"Oh my goodness," the President shrieked, "it's built into that shoe?" The President gawked at the shoe and shuddered.

"Do they come in any other colors?"

Bella rolled her eyes.

I was getting irritated and when I opened my mouth to say something Bella nudged me with her elbow..

"Be respectful," she cautioned in a whisper. I closed my mouth and looked down at the floor.

Bella thought for a moment and was about to say something but she was interrupted by the Vice President's snoring. Everyone turned and glared at the couch.

"Madam President," I changed the subject, "You said you needed us for an emergency." I slipped my shoes back on and said, "How may I help?"

"Oh yeah... that," the President replied.

"As you may know, our sun is just one star among billions of stars in the Milky Way Galaxy and the Milky Way Galaxy is just one of millions of galaxies in the universe."

"Yes I know Madam President," I replied calmly, wondering where the President was going with this. I glanced at Bella but Bella simply shrugged.

"Well..." the President continued, "our scientists have been observing a star named "51 Pegasi" since 1995. At 50 light years away it's the closest star to our solar system that has planets in orbit around it. They've discovered a planet very similar to earth revolving around the star. They named the planet '51 Pegasi C' since it's the third planet in orbit around 51 Pegasi. Get it 1-2-3, a-b-c."

"This is all very interesting, but I don't believe you woke me up to give me an astronomy lesson, did you?"

"Of course not," the President said defensively. "Are you aware of the S.E.T.I. program?" The President asked.

"I've heard of it," I admitted "The Search for Extra Terrestrial Intelligence is what the acronym stands for I believe."

"That's right... the S.E.T.I. program consists of many many antenna dishes aimed at distant planets in an effort to detect signals from them as an indication of intelligent life."

"Yes, I know of it, they are listening for "pure tones" that only radio transmissions could produce. These radio signals cannot be generated by nature so their existence must indicate intelligent life," I said.

The President stared at me blankly. "OK... if you say so," she finally said.

"Anyway, years ago our scientists intercepted a transmission but they have not been able to decode it. I was hoping you would take a crack at it with your super computer."

"I'd be happy to," I said, "but I'm still a little confused... what's the emergency?"

"Well you see our scientists are divided when it comes to interpreting the message and the intention of the beings that sent it. Like I said before, the transmission was heavily coded. After all these years, we have only been able to decode a very small portion of it." The President took on a grave demeanor before speaking again.

"There are some who believe the message is from beings hostile to our planet and are planning an invasion. Otherwise why would it be necessary to have such sophisticated encryption?

"There are others, however, who believe the planet 51 Pegasi C is Heaven, the same Heaven talked about in the Bible."

***

Chapter 6

"**Heaven?**" **both Bella** and I asked at the same time.

"Yes, Heaven... now the problem is Russia and China have just learned of the existence of 51 Pegasi C and the message.

"For years they have been experimenting with a machine that would solve our pollution problem. Since planet Earth is the only planet in the universe that was known to be inhabited, their solution is to transport our pollution to one of the uninhabited planets. They have designed and are in the process of building such a machine.

"Many of them don't believe in GOD or Heaven. They believe the transmission is military in nature. Their solution is to destroy the planet rather than risk an invasion. And with the discovery of 51 Pegasi C, their focus has shifted to developing the machine as a weapon.

As soon as the machine is finished, they will use it to attack the planet and render it uninhabitable... killing everyone. We need answers before they finish their weapon. I need you to crack this code as soon as possible.

"However, if an invasion is imminent, I would like to know also for obvious reasons."

"You want to beef up our defenses, right?" Bella asked.

"No silly, I need to get all of my shopping done," she said. "What does one wear to an invasion anyway?"

Bella was so shocked at the president's answer, she started gagging and coughing, I patted her on the back.

"I will do my best," I assured the President.

***

SECTION #6

So when the new president asked for my help, I said yes. The first step was to travel to Canada and talk to this scientist guy.

Now tell me if this sounds dumb to anyone else but me. I have a nuclear powered, one of a kind, flying car. I received special permission from the Congress just to fly it. But Canada is a nuclear free zone, so the nuclear powered car is out of the question. I have a pair of shoes with a teleportation device built-in to them, but their batteries were going dead from the trip to DC and back. I put them on the charger. So with our teleporting shoes at home on the charger we needed to catch a flight to Canada where this scientist dude lives. I had to get my mom to drive me to the airport. My mom also had to hire a town car and arranged for it to take us from the airport to the scientist guy's house and back to the airport.

Now here's the dumb part, I can fly a nuclear powered flying car, I can teleport myself directly into the Oval Office but I'm not allowed to drive a car because I don't have a Driver's License.

Dumb... Right?

Well at any rate... the meeting with the scientist Noel Haire went well. But things got weird on the way home when we stopped to eat. Because for no apparent reason, the restaurant across the street blew up.

***

Chapter 7

"THIS WON'T TAKE long," I told the driver and I asked him to wait for us in front of the house of well known scientist Dr. Noel Haire. He smiled and assured us that he would be waiting because he had been hired for the whole day.

The modest house was tucked away in a secluded valley on the banks of a three mile wide lake.

"Dr. Haire... Doctor Noel Haire," I greeted the doctor through his screen door. He was a short thin man with an upturned nose and very serious, thoughtful eyes.

"Yes, yes, pleased to meet you," the doctor said as he pushed the door open and invited us in.

"Noel Haire," Bella chuckled quietly. "Try saying that five times real fast."

That earned her an elbow in the arm.

"Ow!" Bella cried out. Dr. Haire turned around and looked at us quizzically. I put on my best innocent face, Bella was still rubbing her arm.

"Sooo... you believe that you have found Heaven? Can you explain why?" I asked the doctor before he could ask what was going on.

He shrugged and invited us to sit on the couch.

As soon as Dr. Haire turned his back, Bella gave me a shove and I flew forward and face planted on the couch. Bella hurried over and sat down next to me while ignoring my "you are so going to pay for that" look. If the Doctor noticed us goofing off, he didn't show it. He took a seat across from us.

"First of all, you should know that most of the experts who are analyzing this message disagree with me," he began. His face was expressive and his hands moved constantly while he talked.

"Yes we know," I told him.

"Yes, yes of course... nevertheless I am convinced this message is an ancient language that hasn't been spoken on Earth for thousands of years more accurately I believe it's the language of Adam and Eve. Allow me to explain."

"Of course doctor, please continue," I said.

"For the last ten years scientists have been gathering DNA from people all over the world. Every sample taken so far contains genetic markers that trace back to a small tribe of Bushmen who to this day live in Africa. The language in this message is very similar to the language spoken by these Bushmen.

"Our ancestors migrated from Africa into Europe, Asia and Russia, eventually crossing the Bering Straight into the Americas. I believe that this "migration" happened when God scattered mankind after the tower of Babel... look, look," Dr. Haire said eagerly as he picked up his bible.

"Genesis 11:1... Now the whole world had one language and a common speech. So you see," Dr. Haire continued, "that was when the people of ancient Earth tried to build the Tower that could reach all the way to Heaven and the Lord noticed."

"Next read Genesis 11:8 & 9... So the Lord scattered them from there over all the earth and they stopped building the tower. That is why it was called Babel – because the Lord confused the language of the whole world."

"That's amazing," Bella said. "Archeologists believe Noah's Ark came to rest somewhere in North Africa. If Noah's Ark did land in North Africa it makes sense that humanity could be genetically traced back to the spot where the survivors of the flood landed."

"Exactly," Dr. Haire said excitedly.

I was unable to hide my growing skepticism. I asked, "How can an ancient earth language be coming from a planet so far away?"

Dr. Haire said, "That's why I think this planet is Heaven. It stands to reason that in Heaven they would speak the language of Adam and Eve. My theory is that the language in this message is the language spoken by Adam and Eve before the flood, before the Tower of Babel. The Bushmen are descendants of Noah and we are all descendants of the Bushmen, DNA proves it. Over the years the language of the Bushmen evolved. That's why it's different from the message we received but in some ways it's the same."

"Is it possible the signal you are receiving is a transmission originally from planet earth that's being bounced off 51 Pegasi C somehow?" I asked.

"Absolutely not!"

"Why not?"

"A round trip for this type of signal would take thousands of years. That pre-dates the invention of the transmission equipment."

"What about the theory that the message was sent by a hostile planet that is preparing an invasion?" I asked.

"Nonsense... the first part, the part I decoded reads more like an opening of a speech not a military pre-invasion communication."

"Then why go through all the trouble of encoding a non-military message?" Bella asked. "Most of the military people we spoke to agree that the only reason to encode so much information would be to hide their intentions, which indicates a full scale invasion may be imminent."

***

Chapter 8

"I DON'T BELIEVE it's encryption at all," the doctor said as he moved to the edge of his seat. "What they are calling encryption, I believe, is just a phase variance caused by the differences in the alien broadcast equipment and our receiving equipment," the doctor explained. "I have compensated for that and I have come up with a recording of the entire message in the ancient language... I just don't know enough of the language to make a complete translation."

"I see," I said thoughtfully.

We spoke to the doctor for several more minutes. When it was time to leave we took a copy of the original transmission and Dr. Haire's adjusted version back to our laboratory for analysis.

***

When we walked outside I couldn't shake the feeling that I was being watched. Things were getting weird since we were given this case and that small still voice that my mother explained to me was the Holy Spirit was telling me to be careful.

There was a different car and driver waiting for us. The new driver explained that our original driver had to leave unexpectedly for a family emergency and he had been dispatched to pick us up. There was something in my spirit that was making me uneasy about this new driver.

***

The ride back to the airport was going smooth enough until Bella's stomach started growling. The driver said he knew of a Mckinley's Colossal Burgers just up the road.

We stopped at a Mckinley's because Bella was sure she would die soon if she didn't get something to eat. The restaurant was in a strip of shops and restaurants on the highway, in the middle of nowhere. We were only about a half mile away from the airport so I dismissed the driver, telling him we would walk the rest of the way to the airport after we ate.

We were standing on the sidewalk in front of Mckinley's. Bella could smell the food and was starting to salivate. That was when I saw our driver park and walk behind Mckinley's.

(That's weird.)

"Don't go in there," the toothless homeless woman told us. I hadn't noticed anyone in front of the restaurant at first; this lady had come out of nowhere.

(Weird thing number two.)

"Don't eat at Mckinley's it's bad for you, why don't you eat at Kelly's Kountry Kitchen across the street, foods' much better there."

I turned to see what Bella thought and Bella simply shrugged that she really didn't care. When I turned around to thank the lady she was gone. I looked up and down the highway but she was nowhere to be seen.

(That was weird thing number three.)

Minutes later we were sitting at a window table, waiting for our food at Kelly's. Our waitress, Lori, was an aspiring actress. Someone told Lori that I was the great granddaughter of Paula Abdul. I looked over at Bella, she was rolling on the floor, cracking up.

(Yeah, I wonder who could have done it?)

Bella swore it wasn't her...

(Yeah... Right!)

So naturally Lori felt compelled to audition for me.

(Oh gag... Maybe it's not too late to eat at Mckinley's)

Mercifully the audition ended and our food arrived. I was having a tuna sandwich and Bella was having a double deluxe grease burger. And just as I started to take a bite of my sandwich... I happened to glance out the window. I saw our driver drive by, our eyes met... he was surprised to see us at the Kountry Kitchen, I could see it register on his face... and then Mckinley's Burgers across the street exploded.

(If you didn't count the singing waitress, that was weird thing number four, which is one more weird thing than allowed.)

***

SECTION #7

I mean... I am not normally a squeamish person. But when we stopped to eat at Kelly's Kountry Kitchen and McKinley's Burgers, the restaurant across the street blew up. And we came within an ant's eyebrow of being "IN" the blown up restaurant and being blown up too... that got my attention.

(There is only one possible conclusion to be drawn... Canadian food is bad for you)

But get this, after McKinley's blew up, Bella shrugged it off and gobbled down her food anyway. Like nothing happened. When I told her I had lost my appetite, she shrugged and gobbled down my food too. She was about to lick the plates when I dragged her out.

(Unbelievable)

We made it home without further incident and we were more motivated than ever. We got right to work on analyzing the message. We worked on decoding the message almost non-stop for almost two weeks. And after the computer failed we decided to solve the problem with a new and completely radical approach.

✳✳✳

Chapter 9

Two Weeks Later

BELLA AND I huddled around the monitor and watched as the powerful computer analyzed the transmission. But, even my computer, as powerful as it was, didn't make much progress.

"Something is wrong, it should be finished by now. I should scan the computer for a virus to be sure," Bella said.

Just as Bella started the scan for viruses, alarms started to sound. Both Bella and I stared at the monitor and then we knew.

"Cyber attack!" Bella shouted, "Someone is trying to break through our fire wall and they are very good. They had to be to even get this far."

We were losing the battle to block the hackers, it soon became clear we were going to have to shut the computer down to protect it.

"I guess that explains the lack of progress. Something or someone does not want us to crack this code. The virus was designed to slow the computer down, and once it got in, it would erase the memory," Bella said.

"Now what," I said, "without the computer we will never crack the code.

Bella was quiet; I could tell something was on her mind. She said,

"I don't believe this message is in code, so I don't believe the computer would have cracked it anyway." Bella swung her chair around to face me and said, "I think it's a presentation like Dr. Haire said. I agree with the doctor, this message could not have originated on earth. But as far as this transmission being a message that was somehow broadcast from Heaven; I don't buy it."

"Explain to me what you're thinking Bella," I insisted. I stopped looking at the monitor and tried to read Bella's face.

Bella collected her thoughts and said, "Number one, I believe Heaven exists in the spiritual realm so it doesn't make sense that Heaven would be a planet we could see with our eyes. Number two... I would be very disappointed if I got to Heaven and we used radios to communicate."

"What we really need is to find out more about the planet. I would hate for our planet to be judged on a single radio transmission... what if right now they are looking at one of our broadcasts of the Jersey Shore?"

I said, "Well, we wouldn't have to worry about an invasion. They wouldn't want to have anything to do with us."

"Yeah or they would just nuke us from space," Bella agreed.

***

When I have a good idea, I mean a really good idea it's hard for me to stay cool and that's what happened this time. I jumped to my feet and announced, "Why don't we send a rover robot, like the one on mars, to the planet and check it out?"

(Ta-da!)

"I like that idea," Bella said excitedly. Then her enthusiasm disappeared just as quickly, "the only problem is the trip would take about ten years even with the new Quantum rocket engines you invented last week. Our robot would arrive after the doomsday weapon destroyed the ecosystem and killed everyone on the planet."

"We could use the teleportation machine," I suggested.

"Won't work boss... the machine isn't powerful enough to transport us to the planet," Bella observed.

"Yeah, but I bet it could be re-configured to send a machine... what do you say to building a new teleporter and adapt it to the rover robot? With the teleporter we could have the rover on 51 Pegasi c in less than an hour."

"It's possible... let's do it," Bella said enthusiastically.

***

SECTION #8

We decided to send a probe using a modified transporter. We worked on it for a week. We were amazed at the speed in which the ideas came. I had been "inspired" in my work before, but never like this. Problems were resolved almost as quickly as they presented themselves.

Finally, our work was complete. After the transporter powered up, Bella activated the controls that would send the rover robot to the planet 51 Pegasi C.

The robot vibrated and beeped, it shimmered in the light then it disappeared into a small vortex of blue and white flashing light.

We laughed and did our victory dance. Tired smiles and high fives lasted much longer than it should have. We had no way of knowing that soon we would have a most unexpected visitor and our lives would never be the same.

✳✳✳

Chapter 10

"**WELL THAT'S DONE,**" Bella said, collapsing back into her chair. "It will take about an hour for the rover to arrive and about twenty-four hours for the video signal to reach us."

"Twenty-four hours seems like an awfully long time," I said as I stood and stretched. "What about the enhancements we made in the transmission equipment?"

"The enhancements are the reason it will only take twenty four hours. Without them we would get a response in about five years," Bella said.

"It's been a long week," I said as I stood and started putting away my tools, "let's get some rest."

***

That night I lay in my bed trying to sleep, but sleep would not come. I couldn't understand how I could be so tired but still have trouble sleeping, but I was and I did. I tossed and turned until I finally gave up and traded my tossing and turning for pacing the floor.

Maybe I was still jumpy from the creepy Canadian driver or the fact that a disappearing bag lady saved us from getting blown up.

Could it be the cyber attack on our computer? Or possibly it was just that feeling I was being watched that I couldn't shake.

***

I was in my room pacing a hole in my carpet when I happened to glance out of my bedroom window. I saw a man in a long coat standing across the street in the shadows, smoking a cigarette. He was tall and thin, wearing a hooded sweat shirt beneath his coat. The hood was pulled up over his head. He turned and looked up at my window and the streetlights briefly illuminated his face. He was movie star handsome but his mouth was twisted in a menacing smirk.

I was about to go outside and confront him. I wanted to find out who he was and why he was watching my window.

Be careful,

That small still voice told me. Instead I went into the living room and told my mom and she called the police but by the time they arrived the man was gone.

The clock read 8:00 PM when I got back to my room afterwards. I felt compelled to pray, so that's exactly what I did. I dropped to my knees and began to pray. I remembered praying during the night and somehow my praying became sleeping and sleeping became dreaming.

***

In my dream, I was standing on a hill covered by dead and dying knee-high grass. The sky above was a hazy, dirty brown. The hill was overlooking a vast, flourishing, green valley. Across the valley was another hill covered by lush green grass. I saw someone, a man, standing on the other hill. There are three bright spheres circling above his head. The spheres were so bright, I couldn't make out the features on the man's face. He just stood there and watched as I started to float across the valley towards him.

***

The sound of my mom knocking on my door, woke me up. I rolled over and looked at the clock, it read 10:00 PM.

(Well two hours is better than nothing.)

I looked over at Bella's bed and it was empty.

My mom knocked again and said, "Michelle... Bella just called down, she said that the robot has arrived and that she is receiving preliminary data."

***

Chapter 11

"**TELL HER I'LL** be right there!" I said.

I stepped out of my room into the hallway.

My mother met me in the hallway and asked, "Are you going to eat something before you go up to the attic?" It wasn't until that moment that I realized I hadn't eaten. In fact I couldn't remember the last time I ate something. When we sat down to eat I told my mother about my dream.

"What do you think it means?"

"I don't know honey."

I lowered my head and spoke quietly, "Do you think it was dad, do you think he was trying to tell me something?"

Mom put down her fork and looked into my eyes.

"You know, not a day goes by since your father disappeared that I don't think about him. But I'm sure he's desperately trying to get back to us wherever he is," she paused before she reached across the table and took my hand, "I think he would be proud to know that you stepped in and continued his work in his absence. And since Bella's mom is dead, I know your dad would be pleased that we took Bella in to look after her until he and Bella's father returned.

"I don't know if this dream has anything to do with him or not, but I know you will figure it out, you are good at that kind of stuff because you are special... just like your father."

I was close to tears when I said, "I can figure out so many things but not where he is."

"The answers will come in time," my mother said, "I'm sure of it; we just have to have faith. We will keep digging for the truth and praying for wisdom and we will have our answer when it's time... in GOD's time."

***

Within minutes I was standing in my control center in the attic of my house.

I watched Bella work for a minute and said, "That was quick... I thought you said it would take twenty four hours?"

Bella looked sideways at me while she tapped on the keyboard.

"You're kidding right?"

"No... I could have sworn you told me it would take twenty four hours before we received a signal."

"It did take twenty four hours. You've been asleep all this time... you were sleeping so soundly I decided not to wake you."

Bella began pushing buttons trying to stabilize the signal. I was in shock.

(That can't be true.)

"Earth to Michelle."

"What?"

"Snap out of it, we have work to do."

"OK... I'm with you." I took my seat at the console next to hers and began working with her to stabilize the signal.

"Remember now," Bella cautioned, "whatever we see is going to be at least twenty four hours old."

When the signal stabilized, Bella put the image on the large view screen overhead so that we both could watch. Initially the image was out of focus but when it cleared up we were looking at a beautiful green landscape and the bluest sky I had ever seen.

Suddenly, without warning, a large shadow darkened the image on the screen and then the signal stopped and the video ceased. Bella tried several times to re-establish contact but it was no use, nothing worked, the robot probe was lost.

"What happened?" I asked as I sat down at the control panel working the controls.

"Don't know boss," Bella responded as she also wrestled with the controls. "It's like, it just... disappeared."

It was the crackling noise that initially got our attention and then a brilliant light exploded into the control room behind us. We spun around to face it. The light was so bright we had to shield our eyes. As the lighting returned to normal, a man stood in the control room in the center of what had been the blinding light moments ago. There was a glowing, basketball size, sphere hovering above his head which seemed to be the source of the light. His eyes were a striking deep green, unlike any I had seen on earth.

He stood well over seven feet tall, thin and fit. His skin was a medium brown, almost orange in color. His hair was dark brown with streaks of blue. He wore an ankle length robe which was the exact same color as his eyes. Yet, there was something almost regal about him.

***

The intruder smiled warmly and spoke. "Do not be afraid... I mean you no harm."

(Yeah right, that's what the invading aliens always said in every science fiction movie I have ever seen.... just before they attacked!)

I inched my finger close to the alarm button, the alarm button which would have put the attic control room on lock down and alerted the military. I was about to push it, but then a quiet-still voice encouraged me not to.

Be still, I am with you.

"Who are you and how did you get past my security?" I demanded.

"You can call me Aaron for now. I come from 'Pardes' the planet you call 51 Pegasi C. I discovered your device and modified it to bring me here," Aaron said.

"Why are you here?" Bella inquired.

"Why did you send the device?" Aaron asked, answering Bella's question with a question. I was becoming suspicious because it seemed that "Aaron," whoever he was, was avoiding the questions. I was about to challenge him on this but again I heard that small still voice.

Answer him

"We intercepted your transmission. We were unclear as to its nature. We sent the probe to investigate," I explained.

Aaron's eyes changed from green to a deep purple and each time his eyes changed his robe changed colors to match. "Transmission? Show me," Aaron requested calmly. I signaled Bella to replay the message. It spilled out from the speaker as a series of beeps and buzzing separated by static. Aaron's eyes and robe changed to yellow, then orange as he listened.

"That does not sound like anything I have ever heard on my planet before," Aaron said.

Then I had an idea. "Can you play the second recording, the one with the phase adjustment," I asked Bella.

Bella typed a few keystrokes and the second version spilled from the speakers. Aaron's eyes retreated to its original green color.

"That I recognize," Aaron said.

"So you're telling me you can understand this language?"

"I should... the person speaking happens to be me."

Bella and I must have looked skeptical so Aaron felt compelled to explain further.

"The transmission is in my native tongue. In fact this is the language I am speaking at this moment."

"But we can understand you now," Bella observed.

"That is because I am using an electronic translator... you have different languages on your planet do you not?"

"Yeah," Bella answered cautiously.

"And you have human translators who listen to one language, translate it in their minds and then speak another, right?"

"Yeah, I guess."

"Well my device works in the same fashion only electronically and almost instantaneously. The device also takes your words and instantly translates them into my language."

I noticed a device in Aaron's ear that somewhat resembled a cell phone's Bluetooth headset. It was then that I noticed that Aaron's lips didn't match his words. It was like watching a movie dubbed in English that had been filmed in another language.

Aaron reached up and touched a device, deactivating the translator. Then he said,

"♎ ⟋ ⅄ ≋ *er* ℳ ♌)(♋ ℳ ❖ ō; r ondræ rouz säz)(♋ ℳ ❖."

To me, Aaron's language sounded exactly like the adjusted transmission. I began to pace while I assimilated this information, it was starting to make sense now. Aaron touched the device and reactivated his translator.

"There are some on this planet who believe this message to be a prelude to war between our worlds," I said.

"Oh no, far from it... this transmission is over a thousand years old. It's a sermon I delivered to the faithful. It was the first ever transmission to be broadcast around our world. It makes sense that it would be the first that you would receive," Aaron explained.

"OK... let's say I decide to accept your explanation... for now. I need you to accompany me to meet with our President. We need to prevent a war."

"I am sorry, but I am not permitted to leave this room. I am not to interact in any way with your world, nor am I to speak to anyone else but you."

"Why not?" Bella asked.

"It's difficult to explain," Aaron said.

"Then why are you here?" I repeated Bella's earlier question.

"Our Father has sent me on a mission of vital importance."

"Our Father?"

"The One, the Alpha and Omega."

Both Bella and I looked at one another in disbelief.

Aaron pointed to the sphere and said, "This device is set to return us to my planet automatically. We don't have much time. Our Father has sent me to bring you back with me to 'Pardes'... prepare yourselves."

"What are you talking about... "

Before I could finish my question I saw a vortex of flashing light appear and I felt myself being pulled in. I looked around in time to see Bella grabbing hold to her chair. Then the world around me blinked out.

***

SECTION #9

Our visitor, Aaron, took us to his planet in a blink of an eye.

(Well technically we were kidnapped, but neither of us was complaining. Especially when he told us that GOD told him to do it. How can you argue with that one?)

I once saw a hologram of a beautiful forest that once existed on Earth and as real as the hologram seemed, it paled in comparison to reality. It was so beautiful, I almost cried. And even though it was a completely alien planet in every way, I had the strange feeling that I was coming home for the first time.

(Weird huh?)

It was so beautiful on Pardes, so green, more green than I imagined possible.

(Aaron explained to us that our testimony was needed to keep it that way)

✳✳✳

Chapter 12

WE WERE STANDING in the deep green grass of a vast flourishing green plain. Across the plain, I could see a glowing crystal city sparkling on a hill surrounded by a beautiful forest complete with flora and fauna unlike anything I had ever seen before.

"Where are we?" I asked.

"We are on 'Pardes'. There is a similar word in your Hebrew language that means 'Orchard'. But I think this can better be described by what a similar place was once called on your planet... the Garden of Eden," Aaron said in a calm voice. His eyes flashed red but quickly returned to the previous deep green color.

"I don't understand," I said.

"Our Father has brought you here to give testimony."

"Testimony?" I exclaimed.

"Let me explain from the beginning, I was walking with the Lord on our daily walk when He showed me your machine. Until then we didn't know you existed. The Father chose that moment to explain that He created other worlds, other Gardens of Eden, other Adams and other Eves.

"On your world Adam and Eve ate the fruit from the 'Tree of

Knowledge of Good and Evil' and caused your world to fall," Aaron explained.

"So are you telling me, that you are Adam?" Bella asked.

"No, as I said before my name is Aaron... well that's not exactly the truth. My name is "χÊΨŽØα" but 'Aaron' is as close as we are going to get in your language. Our Adam and Eve lived to be four thousand years old. They went to Heaven many years ago after they died."

"They went to Heaven? You mean this isn't it?"

"Oh geez, no... from what the Father tells me this world is like a trash heap compared to Heaven."

I said, "It's so beautiful here, more so than anything I've ever seen. There is nothing to compare to this on our planet... It's paradise!"

"Our planet has existed for millions of years much the way you see it now," Aaron said as he looked out upon the countryside. "But there's trouble in paradise. Lucifer is here and he is causing trouble."

"Lucifer! Here!" Bella shouted. She began scanning the area as if Lucifer would jump out from behind a tree and attack at any moment.

"Yeah he's around... he's one of those self-absorbed, egotistic guys... if you know what I mean. He's all wrapped up in himself, always combing his hair, making sure he looks good. He can't pass a mirror without checking himself out.

"He's always around, saying crazy things. Usually people just ignore him because he has no power here." Aaron leaned closer, "he's a fallen angel, managed to get his butt kicked out of Heaven. But, the Father said that it's better if we don't know the details. I do know that he's afraid of Mychal the Arch Angel," Aaron said with a laugh. "Whenever he gets to be a bother we just command him to go in the Name of the Father and he takes off."

"So what's the problem?" Bella asked.

"Unfortunately Lucifer has convinced three nitwits that if they were to eat of the 'Tree of Knowledge of Good and Evil', they would be as powerful as the Lord himself. They went and found themselves a lawyer. The three plaintiffs have brought a petition to the Supreme Planetary Council of judges to demand the right to eat the forbidden fruit."

I considered this information for a moment.

"I know what happened when the first man and woman on our planet ate of the 'Tree of Knowledge of Good and Evil'. They were thrown out of the garden and all of their descendants were cursed and lived thereafter in a fallen state. But that opportunity on this world has passed. Surely GOD would not condemn the entire planet for the actions of three people," I said.

Aaron nodded thoughtfully and said, "you have a good point, no one knows for sure. I imagine the offenders could be cast out. Our Garden of Eden now covers the entire planet, but it wasn't always that way. There used to be an exit to the garden, a way out and there were a couple of tough looking angels with flaming swords keeping whatever was outside the garden from coming in. But now that the garden covers the entire planet, if someone was cast out they would have to go somewhere else."

"I wonder where?" Bella asked idly.

Aaron didn't answer he just looked away and then it hit me like a slap in the face.

"Earth," I said.

Aaron nodded, "the Lord told me yesterday when he told me your planet existed. Our kind can survive on your world so those who have been expelled from the garden in the past have been sent to Earth."

(But there was something else, I could feel it, something Aaron isn't telling me and it has something to do with my dad. Suddenly I knew, and a big piece to the puzzle fell into place.)

We all stood there in silence until Bella spoke.

"Is the tree guarded?" Bella asked.

"Well, actually no, it is not. The tree is in a plaza in front of the great Hall. Anyone can get to it," Aaron said.

"So why don't they just go and eat and be done with it?" I asked.

"I don't know, I never thought about it. There are very few people on this planet that think the way you do," Aaron said.

"What do you mean?" Bella asked.

"No offence, but deception and breaking the rules are unknown to us."

"None taken," Bella said.

"It may be that people don't simply go up to the tree and pick the fruit because it's against the rules," Aaron confessed. "But I think I know why the plaintiffs don't just do it on their own."

"Really, what are you thinking," I asked.

"The fact that some have been expelled from the garden in our history tells me that it's possible. I have to assume that Lucifer has been able to deceive others and convinced them to eat the forbidden fruit. I think that you are right Michelle, GOD would not condemn the entire world for the actions of just a few and Lucifer won't be satisfied with just those three.

"That may explain why Lucifer insisted that the lawyer present the case to the council. If the council as representatives of the entire planet made a choice to eat of the tree, perhaps then it would condemn the entire planet. I'm just not sure what all of the repercussions will be if the decision is to eat the forbidden fruit.

"I am responsible for defending the planet's decision not to eat of the tree. I was preparing arguments for a hearing before the Supreme Council of Judges. That is when your probe showed up and it took every scientist on the planet, working together around the clock to modify your equipment to send me to Earth and bring you back."

"That's weird," I said.

"It gets weirder; there was another scientist who happened to be working on a translator because he wanted to talk to the animals. As stewards of this planet he felt we should get their input. He had been working on the translation technology for years.

"Think about that for a minute. We needed a witness that cannot be found anywhere on this planet, suddenly we have the technology to locate you and bring you here and also the means to communicate. Everything just fell into place. I refuse to believe that all of this was just a coincidence."

"I agree," I said. "I just recently developed the technology that sent the probe to your planet. I refuse to believe that the timing of the creation of this technology and the hearing at the Supreme Planetary Council is purely coincidental."

Aaron talked some more about the planetary council and the testimony we were being asked to give. Something had been weighing heavy on my heart and now I knew what it was.

"I can't stay," I said, "my dad has recently disappeared and if I was to disappear too, it might be more than my mom can bear."

"The father assures me that he will have someone explain to your mom that you are safe and on a mission for him and you will be home shortly. Michelle we need you, our whole world may be at stake."

We stood listening to Aaron's words, light years from our homes, in the greenest grass we had ever seen. We looked up into a blue smog free sky, bluer than we could have imagined. We breathed in air so clean it almost hurt. For the first time Bella and I realized what we, as inhabitants of Earth, had lost and we knew what we had to do.

"OK, I'm in," I said.

"Count me in too," Bella agreed.

"Good, let's go!" Aaron said before he turned to walk away.

"Ummm, just one thing before we go," Bella said. We followed her eyes and noticed for the first time what she still held in her hands. "What should I do with the chair?" Bella asked.

***

SECTION #10

I tried to describe Aaron's robe to someone later and they told me that what I was describing was a "frock" I didn't even know what a "frock" was. A frock apparently is a sort of baggy, hooded outer garment similar to what a monk on Earth would wear. The only monk I knew was an obsessive compulsive detective in a 25 year old TV show. And when they explained that it was the favored attire of Jedi and Jawa I knew.

(I wonder why they just didn't say that in the first place.)

In the distance I could see a Crystal City on a hill. Aaron informed us that the Crystal City was our destination. We could not have known it but that persistent feeling that we were being watched was true... we were.

✳✳✳

Chapter 13

His frock was glowing an intense bright red. He had to cover it with a handmade black cloth frock, because it would have been impossible to hide in the bushes. His name was Alep and he was assigned to follow the Chief Guardian Aaron. Somehow his boss knew something was going on, but then his boss always knew.

Alep couldn't believe what he was seeing, "Aliens" were here. Until now everyone assumed that they were alone in the universe and now he was the first to know that everyone was wrong. But what did it mean? He had to get back to the city and report his findings. But more importantly he wanted answers, his world was about to change and he had chosen sides. Now he desperately hoped he had chosen the right one.

***

Before we set off, Bella's stomach took the opportunity to start growling. It was loud and long and it startled Aaron who eyed her suspiciously.

"What else have you brought with you? You didn't bring one of those strange earth animals the Father told me about did you?" Aaron asked. We burst out laughing. Aaron's eyes narrowed as they changed from green to orange. He didn't understand the joke.

"Her stomach just growled that's all."

"Why does a stomach growl?"

"Because she's hungry, you came to get us before we had a chance to eat!"

"Then why won't she eat something?" Aaron asked, his eyes turned purple to reflect his confusion.

"Duh... because there isn't a McKinley's Colossal Burger in sight," Bella said jokingly.

"A Mac-a-What???"

"McKinley's is a restaurant, a restaurant is a building that prepares food on our planet it's where we go to get fast food."

"I don't understand the concept of a restaurant, but fast food I understand... you want fast food, watch this," Aaron said confidently as he walked over to the side of the road, bent down and picked up two of many wafers that littered the countryside.

"What's that?" I asked suspiciously.

"Fast food!" Aaron answered as he offered each of us a wafer.

"I'm not eating off the ground," I objected.

"Me neither... that is unless the three second rule is in effect... no, wait, those have been on the ground for way more than three seconds," Bella pointed out.

"Three second rule, what's that?"

"Ignore her or she'll confuse you." I said.

"Well I'm already confused," Aaron said, "they're still good, they evaporate long before they spoil."

"It's not that... it's just... on our planet we don't eat food off the ground."

"Well you're not on your planet... this food comes directly from the Father. You can eat these now or you can wait till we get to the city where you can pick fruit from one of the trees."

Bella eyed the wafer suspiciously. It was about the size of a silver dollar.

"What does it taste like?"

"Whatever you want it to."

"Yeah right, well, I'm hungry. I'm going to need more than one of those itty bitty things!"

Aaron didn't respond. He was too busy rolling his eyes, a trick he picked up from his new friends from Earth. We shrugged then took the offered wafers. After eating just one wafer we were both full and satisfied.

Bella smacked her lips and belched. She immediately covered her mouth and said, "Oh excuse me, but that thing was delicious. It tasted just like a Colossal Double Grease Burger... just the way I remembered it... with a bun and everything!"

"Mine tasted like a vegetable smoothie," I said, "that's amazing, how can you tell the wafers apart?"

"We don't, as I said they taste like whatever you want them to... now I know what vegetables are, I don't understand why anyone would put it in a smoothie," Aaron said.

Bella made her gagging gesture again, I responded with an extremely difficult and rarely attempted double eye roll.

Aaron continued and asked, "But what is a Colossal Double Grease Burger?"

I opened my mouth to explain but stopped myself. It was now obvious to me that the differences between a fallen planet and a planet that had not fallen were too great to comprehend without a common frame of reference.

"It's a F.P.T. you wouldn't understand," was what popped into my head and was what I said.

"F.P.T.?" Aaron asked.

"Yeah, that's right... a F.P.T.," I said with a laugh "A Fallen Planet Thing, you wouldn't understand."

Bella choked out a laugh, Aaron smiled and shrugged.

"I guess that will have to do," he decided. As Aaron turned again to walk away. The ground gave way beneath his feet; he lost his balance and slipped down onto the dusty dirt road. We helped him to his feet. His once sparkling clean robe was covered with dirt. I was about to help him dust himself off, but before I could the dirt just fell away.

"Wow," I said, "How did you do that?"

"Do what?"

"Your robe, the dirt, it just fell off!"

Aaron looked down at his robe and then back at us. "What did you expect?" Aaron asked.

"On our planet the dirt remains, we have to get our clothes washed... cleaned."

"Washed, cleaned?"

"Yeah like in a washing machine."

Aaron burst out laughing, "That's ridiculous. Why would you need a machine for something that happens automatically?"

"Because it doesn't happen automatically where we come from. The machine mixes soap and water and swishes everything together until the clothes are clean," I explained.

"Unless you get them dry cleaned," Bella added.

"Dry? You just said you needed water."

Bella looked at me for help; I crossed my arms and looked the other way.

(You keep digging these holes; I'm not helping you out of
this one.)

"Well dry cleaning does use a little water mixed in with a lot of chemicals... " Bella tried to explain, but Aaron interrupted.

"So if dry cleaning really isn't dry, why do you call it dry cleaning?" Aaron asked.

Bella considered his questions for a moment and saw an escape.

"It's a fallen planet thing," she said.

"I know, I know," Aaron said as he held up his hands in surrender.

"You wouldn't understand!" Bella finished her sentence anyway.

"Abso-posa-lutely," Aaron agreed.

"That's not a word," I said.

"The translator says it is, so it is now!" Aaron insisted with a small triumphant smile.

(He's right, his planet... his rules.)

"We had better get going," Aaron said as he pointed to the sparkling city in the distance.

I looked down towards the city which was our destination. It appeared to be at least ten miles away. I looked up at the sky and estimated that it would be well after dark before we arrived.

***

Lucifer sat in his small office and considered the troubling report he had just received from one of his spies. The Chief Guardian Aaron had gone out to the countryside and literally disappeared only to reappear hours later in the company of two aliens. From the spy's description, Lucifer had no doubt where the aliens were from and he had no doubt as to why they were here. Now he had to figure out what he could do about it.

For now he would deploy a team to meet them at the outskirts of the city and follow them. He had missed his chance to take them out on Earth. He should have blown up both restaurants, but who knew they would change their minds at the last minute on the advice of a homeless lady.

He would decide what to do about the aliens as soon as darkness fell. He was not going to allow either of them to survive long enough to participate in tomorrow's hearing.

***

Chapter 14

WE STARTED WALKING down that dirt road, but after only about six steps we found ourselves standing on the outskirts of the Crystal City.

I froze in my tracks and said, "How did that happen?" How did we get here so fast? We were walking on the hill, I blinked then we were here!"

"I don't know, we just start on our journey and GOD does the rest... it's always been that way," Aaron said as he looked into our startled faces. "Why? How do people get around on your world?"

"Well, Bella and I have a nuclear powered flying car, but the rest of the world uses other forms of transportation."

"Such as?" Aaron asked.

"Cars, trains, boats, bicycles, planes, helicopter... " I said ticking off my fingers.

"Skateboard, dirt bike, horse, Camel, dog sled, Rickshaw..."

Something in Bella's brain told her that now would be a good time for a smart aleck remark so she added the ridiculous to the list, "river tubes, piggyback rides."

I gave her another elbow.

"Ow... that's gonna leave a mark," Bella said.

"You are going to confuse him," I warned before I explained what each one was, leaving out river tubes and piggyback rides.

"That's insane, how do you decide which one to take?"

"Well, it depends on the distance you have to travel," I said thoughtfully, "The amount of time you have to get there."

"And how much money you have," Bella added.

"Money??" Aaron appeared confused.

I took a minute to explain the concept of money to Aaron, simply, as I would to a child.

"My goodness, how can you stand to operate that way?" Aaron almost shouted.

I gave Aaron the fish eye.

Aaron caught himself and said, "Forget I asked... I know it's a fallen world thing!"

I said, "Actually, what I was going to say was that we have no choice. Our world is broken and as bad as it is; at one time it was much much worse. The Lord does not come and walk with us the way He does on your planet. So He sent his son... Jesus to die on the cross to redeem us with his blood. Then He sent his Holy Spirit to live inside us, to help us, so that we could have fellowship with him."

I took a few minutes as we walked through the city to explain to Aaron about the Holy Trinity and the Bible. About how sin entered my world through the actions of Adam and Eve and how Lucifer was allowed to rule since man obeyed him rather than GOD. I spoke about everything I could think of. I finished up with Jesus Christ and how His death on the cross redeemed man. When I finished Aaron simply nodded then he smiled.

"GOD is good, isn't He? He made a way when there was no way... didn't He!"

Bella and I looked at one another and then at Aaron and smiled.

"Abso-posa-lutely!" we both said simultaneously.

***

Our destination was a building Aaron called "The Great Hall." We were getting our first look at the alien city. There were no streets in the Crystal City because there were no cars. The pathways that snaked between the buildings were wide and dedicated to pedestrian traffic.

The walkways were made of the same crystal material as the buildings, but not as hard. It was kinda like walking on the floor of a gymnasium, it was firm, but with just the right amount of give to it. The walkways were a deep blue... its dark color stood in sharp contrast to the white color of the buildings.

The walkways were crowded with people dressed in robes similar to Aaron's. The people interacted as they moved about, the color of their robes changed with the nature of the conversations. We received a few curious glances, but for the most part our strange appearance didn't seem to disrupt the daily flow of activity.

I did begin to notice people appearing and disappearing all around us, no doubt taking advantage of this world's very unique form of mass transit. It kinda freaked me out at first, but I was starting to get used to it. There was something else I noticed. Most of the people on the street had robes that glowed blue, green or an occasional purple. But there were at least three that I picked out of the crowd whose robes were bright red. I didn't know if it meant anything and I made a note to ask Aaron about it. In the meantime I was going to keep my eyes on them.

***

Lamedh and Kaph spread out and kept pace behind the Chief Guardian Aaron just the way their boss had taught them. Zayin had been intercepted and was being prayed for, but would catch up as soon as he could shake the people who insisted on praying for him.

Lamedh watched the strange visitors as they wandered along

the walkway and like everyone else he was curious as to where these strange looking visitors were from.

He and the rest of his group had taken Lucifer's advice and they no longer participated in their daily walks with the Lord so when the Lord told everyone of the aliens' arrival he and his group were out of the loop.

Although he would never admit it to Lucifer, he missed the walks. But it was a small price to pay to someday himself be a God. Lucifer didn't say it, but he hinted that these aliens were here to influence the hearing. He felt his anger flare as he thought about being denied God's power, anger that he was learning to direct at the visitors.

Lamedh had spoken with some contacts who were still walking with the Lord and learned that the two aliens were visiting 'Pardes' from another planet but no one fully understood why. There was a lot of speculation, but no one truly knew.

Besides him, his crew consisted of Kaph and Zayin and they were instructed to simply watch the Chief Guardian and his new friends and report back. They had to take turns following so as to not draw too much attention. Lamedh's biggest problem occurred when people noticed the red robes of his crew, they would stop them and pray with them thinking them in some kind of distress. When one of his crew was peeled off by helpful pedestrians, another would step in and take up the surveillance. Only they knew it wasn't distress but a growing anger towards the visitors, towards Aaron, towards God.

∗∗∗

SECTION #11

Aaron thought it was important for us to see where we would be testifying. And before long we stood outside of our destination, the "Great Hall." The enormity of the structure took our breath away.

The Great Hall was practically hidden between the mile high skyscrapers we had been passing between. But its unique construction made it stand out from the other much taller but generally identical buildings. The Great Hall was at least as tall as the Empire State Building, but with a wide domed top. The entire building resembled a gigantic mushroom. It was angular, however, cut like a giant diamond. It was constructed of a semi-clear crystalline material that seemed to absorb the surrounding light and distribute it internally, making the entire structure glow.

Chapter 15

"OUR PLANET IS essentially one huge garden. The Garden is divided into 490 districts. There is a city like this one in each of the districts and one judge per city. Occasionally minor disputes arise and the judges are responsible for making decisions to resolve those issues. But typically the judges remind them of their obligation to practice forgiveness and turning the other cheek. Usually the petty squabbles will disappear and the disagreements are solved long before the council can meet and render a verdict.

"490... 70 x 7?" I asked rhetorically. Aaron did the math. "Yeah, I guess so, does that mean something?" Aaron asked.

"Yeah, but don't worry about it," I said.

"At any rate, the judges always meet in this hall and the next meeting is set for tomorrow at dawn," Aaron said.

Just as Aaron finished talking, something flew by just above Bella's head and it startled her. We hadn't noticed many birds since we had arrived on this planet even when we were in the country, in fact there hadn't been anything flying. But now that I thought about it there weren't many birds at home either.

Bella's eyes tracked the soccer ball sized polished metallic sphere as it zoomed away. It was a much smaller version of the sphere Aaron used to bring us here. What was it doing here, I wondered. And why hadn't Aaron told us about it. My first thought was that it was some kind of surveillance device, but why would you need surveillance in paradise?

***

Chapter 16

I **LOOKED UP,** following Bella's eyes.

And then followed the sphere with my eyes as it climbed. A quick gasp slipped from my mouth as I saw it join a swarm of thousands of spheres. They raced around in the sky overhead. The spheres were flashing different colors with pinpoint sized lights covering each sphere. Hundreds of lights of red, blue, green and purple that reminded me of Christmas tree lights, moved across and around each sphere. The spheres flashed different colorful patterns each time they came into close proximity of another.

"What are those," I asked.

Aaron looked up and spotted what had drawn our attention.

"Each person on the planet has one. They are constantly moving about gathering news, delivering and receiving greetings, messages, whatever. Upon demand, it delivers its messages directly to our minds. Of course we get a lot of our information during our daily walks with the Lord."

Aaron knew he would regret it but he had to ask, "How do you communicate on your world?"

"Twitter, FaceBook, blogs," Bella said.

"Cell phones, Internet, newspapers, e-mails, text messages," I added.

Bella stepped out of elbow range and added a sarcastic, "Smoke signals," to the list.

"My goodness, how do you know which one to check?"

"You have to constantly check them all. Sometimes one system will alert you to check the other one."

"Now that just sounds dumb. You're joking right?"

"It's a..."

"I know... Wow... What does a headache feel like, I think I'm getting one," Aaron groaned. We laughed out loud.

"How does that work?" Bella asked.

"The spheres? Don't know, it's... technology, I don't understand how any of this technology works, I just know that it does."

"No not that, go back to something you said before, the daily walks with the Lord. There aren't enough hours in the day for one on one walks with millions of people. Even if he walked with one whole district at a time there are 490 of them. He can't walk with everyone."

"But he does," Aaron said proudly.

"How?" Bella asked.

"Don't know... He just does, he's God!"

"I'm not following," Bella said as she scratched her head.

Aaron thought for a moment, then he prayed, then he smiled and began to explain.

"The father told me that in your Bible it is written that: 'whenever two or more of you are gathered in my name, there I am in the midst of thee.' I'm sure that there is more than one such meeting occurring on your world at any given time. So if he can do that he can do individual daily walks."

"That makes sense," I said sticking my tongue out at Bella as I agreed with Aaron.

"I still don't get it," Bella said.

"I have walked with the Lord and have spoken with people I know and trust who also insist they have been walking with the Lord at the same time, so I have no doubt it happens. So I guess you are just going to have to take my word for it on that one because there is no way that I can prove it to you."

"Yeah Bella, quit being such a 'Doubting Thomas'."

"Doubting Thomas, what's that?"

"A 'Doubting Thomas' is kinda like a hater."

"Hater?"

"Never mind."

"No, no tell me I want to know what a hater is." Aaron insisted.

Bella and I were grinning and nodding in agreement.

"It's a... " Bella started to say.

"Oh be quiet," Aaron snapped playfully.

We all couldn't help but laugh hysterically.

***

When we reached the Great Hall, I immediately spotted the plaza that Aaron had told us about. The 'Tree of Life' and the 'Tree of the Knowledge of Good and Evil' were growing in the open patch of earth in the plaza out in front of the Great Hall, in the middle of the city, in the middle of a Garden Planet. I looked at the two large trees. I'm not sure what I was expecting, but they looked so ordinary to me.

The sound of the doors opening caught us all by surprise. A dark-haired man dressed in a royal blue traditional sash of the Guardians of the Great hall beckoned and then invited us in.

We were lead down a long corridor, the floor was a blue crystalline substance and it was even softer than the crystalline walkway we had been walking on earlier. The corridor eventually emptied into a cavernous room, "The Great Hall".

The "Great Hall" itself, or... at least the bottom half, reminded me of a stadium on Earth. It looked like it was built to watch something like professional basketball or tennis, except there were only about 500 seats overlooking the floor. The rest of the space was overhead in an enormous open dome designed to accommodate the millions of spheres swirling around inside. The lights from the spheres illuminated the interior crystal walls.

About 1,500 feet above the ground was a large hole at the very top of the dome in the center. When I looked up at the hole, I saw thousands of spheres pouring in to join the millions that were already inside. The spheres swarmed like bees - flashing brilliantly multicolored lights between one another.

Aaron watched the Spheres with us for a moment before he said, "your secret is out, you are the first extra terrestrials this world has ever seen. The Lord has prepared everyone during his daily walks and I guess everyone wants to get a look at you for themselves."

"It's so beautiful," Bella said in awe.

***

Lucifer was in a rage. He stormed around the office smashing everything that couldn't run away. He had planned this operation for more than a thousand years, rigging elections, using the discontent of those who lost to cultivate followers, manipulating the system and for what! He hadn't anticipated that the opposition would be able to come up with witnesses.

"Those witnesses must not testify at the hearing tomorrow," he barked as he dropped angrily into his chair behind his desk. His terrified assistants didn't respond, they simply huddled in a corner and cringed. Reports from his spies were pouring in from all over the

Crystal City. There were aliens on Pardes and the spheres were buzzing with speculation as to why. But he didn't have to speculate, he knew... yes he knew very well. They must not be allowed to speak or his schemes for this world will be ruined.

He looked over at his assistants; he had to be careful with his fits of rage. They had no real concept of anger, though after a thousand or so years of his company they were learning. His biggest problem on this planet was that he didn't have very many followers and it took a thousand years just to cultivate them. This planet was so disgustingly perfect that no one was inclined to even listen to him let alone follow him, unlike on Earth where the nature of the world itself produced followers by the millions. He had made a mistake by not going after the Adam and Eve of 'Pardes' right away, a mistake that he did not repeat when it came to Earth.

His face darkened as he leveled his gaze on the six men and women in the room. "You must go to the house of the Chief Guardian Aaron and bring the aliens to me."

***

SECTION #12

Small cottages could be found throughout the countryside because Crystal City was not for everyone. However, everyone who chose to live in the city lived in mile high skyscrapers made of opaque crystal and light.

There was a startling absence of the normal urban clutter such as street signs, fire hydrants and traffic signals. There were no billboards, no bus stops, no power lines or sewers.

The walkways were wide enough to be divided into three lanes. Foot traffic flowed in both directions in the outer lanes, but the center of the walkway was where all the action was. People were appearing and disappearing in an surprisingly orderly fashion. They appeared blurry at first as if slightly out of focus and once they were fully formed they simply stepped to one side of the walkway or the other.

The sides of the walkways were lined with all kinds of fruit trees and one could simply pick what he or she needed to eat.

There were no honking horns, no sirens were ever heard. Crystal City didn't have a police department because there was no crime. They didn't have a fire department because there was nothing to burn. There was no ambulance service because there were no hospitals, no hospitals because everyone was so disgustingly healthy. Sin had never entered this world, so no one ever got sick. Injuries did however occur, but that was usually quickly remedied by prayer.

We made it to Aaron's house, we were exhausted. And before long we were fast asleep.

That night, the men came for us. And when they couldn't find us, they did the unbelievable.

*****

Chapter 17

WHEN WE EMERGED from the "Great Hall" the sun was beginning to set. The foot traffic had decreased dramatically. And for the first time we got a sense of how quiet the city was. The only sound was the sound of footsteps and gentle crowd chatter. Also there was the soft sound the spheres made while zipping around in the air overhead.

"We will sleep at my home tonight," Aaron announced, "we have a big day ahead of us tomorrow."

Aaron didn't live far from the hall so we decided to walk without the assistance of what Bella had started calling the "HTD" or (Holy Transit District) after Los Angeles' bus system, the "RTD" (Rapid Transit District). As the sun began to disappear, the buildings themselves began to glow, providing soft light for the entire city. The majority of the structures were residences, schools and churches. We passed a number of outdoor theaters and parks and playgrounds but never a shop or a store.

***

The elevator ride up to Aaron's apartment on the 500th floor was quick and quiet.

I was amazed at the technology required to move three people up to the top of a 500 story building in a matter of seconds. I also wondered if the people of 'Pardes' were that much smarter than the people of Earth or was the advanced technology a result of being able to focus their energy towards technology that would benefit the people and not wage war. I also knew that Earth had one advantage over 'Pardes'. If the people of Earth ever attacked this beautiful place it would be no contest. Everyone here seemed so naively peaceful, they would be no match. I thought about the weapon being built and aimed at Pardes at this very moment and the urgency of my mission overwhelmed me to the point I felt sick.

***

The interior of Aaron's apartment was spacious and clean it was made up of six simple rooms, two bedrooms each with an attached bathroom and balcony, a main room and a dining area. The large main room seemed to be designed for group meetings which was understandable because the culture was centered around fellowship and worship.

The walls were composed of a dull white material that was slightly cool to the touch. There were decorations or rather areas on the wall that were painted with a type of abstract art. The colors of the art seemed to change with Aaron's mood.

It occurred to me that Aaron's apartment was more accurately described by what it did not have. Most noticeably, there wasn't a kitchen because on Pardes, no one cooked. No kitchen meant no refrigerator or stove. There were no garbage disposals or garbage cans because people simply didn't create garbage.

Aaron didn't seem to have a big screen television or stereo, only several bean bag style pillows in the sunken center of the main room. And I had yet to see a clock.

There were no heating or air conditioner ducts visible. Aaron said that the weather did change but never to the extremes of summer and winter of Earth. It was a kind of perpetual spring and fall.

There were no light fixtures visible. The interior light was by way of round spots on the ceiling like recessed track lighting. Except for the light pouring from them, the spots were indistinguishable from the rest of the ceiling.

"If you don't have electricity how are we getting light?"

"The lights are made of a special synthetic quartz crystal that stores the sun's energy during the day and provides light during the night." Aaron touched a spot on the wall and the lights dimmed before going off. He touched the spot again and the lights came back on. "We simply cover the quartz crystal to turn off the light. Just about everything is powered by the sun. We never discovered fossil fuels so we directed most of our efforts towards inventing ways to use our sun.

"God brings the rain during the night for a couple of hours to replenish our water supply and irrigate all of the vegetation. Each unit has its own water storage space so the water we need for the day is collected the night before."

"It's just perfect," Bella said, "Everything here works together so perfectly."

"Bella is right, everything is perfect," I said, "I don't get it. Why would anyone want to mess with paradise?"

"There is a dissenting group. They are small but dedicated. They are mostly lawyers and disgruntled politicians who failed to win seats on the Supreme Council. They've spent too many years listening to Lucifer and have become enticed by the promise of God-like power."

"Politicians," I moaned, "they are the same everywhere. They pretend that everything they do is for your benefit but it's always about their selfish needs. On our world we are taught to respect those in authority over us and to even pray for them but it gets hard sometimes."

Meanwhile Bella was noticing a few other things that were missing.

"There are no books," Bella observed.

"We use our spheres for that. We also use them for all of our entertainment needs," Aaron said, "How do you entertain yourselves on your world?"

"3D holographic projectors are the newest thing, but they are expensive. Most people use them to recreate scenes of green grass and trees because almost nothing grows on Earth anymore.

"There is a new device out there called the iChip. For a fee you can have a chip placed directly into your head and you never have to watch a screen or use headphones again, because it feeds music or the movie right into your brain... But there are some side effects."

"Yeah, like people are going crazy," Bella interjected.

"The iChip is supposed to outperform the 'Brain Wave' iPod."

"Yeah, cept if you don't pay your bill they can cut the music off. Every three days you get this annoying voice in your head telling you to pay your bill and if you don't pay, the voice never goes away." Bella added.

"Most people still use the 'Brain Wave' iPods," I said, "it beams the music and video to your brain using a low frequency microwave."

"Yeah, the same microwave beam we use to cook our food, is that crazy or what?" Bella mumbled as she poked at one of Aaron's abstract wall art decorations.

"The 'Brain Wave' iPods replaced the touch iPods, which replaced the CD, which replaced cassette tapes, which replaced the eight track that replaced phonograph records.

"Yeah and before that some dude with a 'lute' traveled from town to town and sang badly in the town square."

"Lute?" Aaron asked confused.

"You'll never learn," I mumbled.

"What on Earth is a Lute?" Aaron asked.

Bella didn't respond she just faked the pee pee dance and ran out of the room.

(Coward!)

"We go to theaters to watch movies," I continued, "unless of course it's out on DVD's. Most movies these days are on the computer. There is cable TV and if you can't afford cable there is regular broadcast TV. We go to libraries to read books. We get magazines delivered to our homes. Nowadays everyone has a Kindle, an iPad or one of those tablets and they can have books, music or movies delivered directly to those devices for a fee.

"We play video games on computers and some people are into playing video games on the Xbox or PS3 or on the internet and they sit and play with people from all over the world for days at a time..."

"Don't forget Reality TV," Bella interrupted as she walked back into the room.

"Stop it, stop it... I'm getting another headache," Aaron was holding his head grimacing, "how in the world do you keep up?"

I gave him a pitying smile and said, "Well don't tell anybody I told you this, but the best way is to jump on the newest fad that comes along because sooner or later everybody will and that way you will always be up to date. I think most of it is harmless, except for the iChip, that is. There is something about having a chip in your brain that just seems stupid to me."

"Too bad, about the books," Bella said, I really would have liked to have read your bible."

"Bible, we don't have a bible," Aaron confessed.

"You don't have a Bible?"

"Nope."

"Why not?" Bella asked.

"I guess because we don't need one. We have history books which are probably the closest thing. Since we never fell we don't need a Bible to tell us how to live. And if we have a question we just ask him during our walk or we can always pray like I just did."

***

Chapter 18

IN THE COUNTRY wafers fell on the ground every day. The animals ate what the people did not. What didn't get eaten by either would dissolve with the nightly rain and become food for the soil. In the city, however, the wafers didn't fall on the ground. Instead each household placed a small basket on their balcony and every morning the number of wafers needed for that household would appear in the basket.

Aaron brought the basket into the dining room, placed it on the table and we all sat down to eat. After Aaron blessed the food, he showed us how to share the taste of our wafer with someone else by imagining what we wanted and then breaking off a piece and passing it around. We got the chance to taste the food from Aaron's planet while Aaron was particularly interested in tasting a "Colossal Double Grease Burger."

Aaron was surprised to see that there was an extra wafer in the basket, but he soon knew why. Bella was a "pig" and God Knew it. Bella embarrassed the entire human race when she pigged out and stuffed herself with two wafers. That made Aaron laugh because he'd never seen anyone eat two wafers before.

After dinner we sat in the main room and talked. I decided to tell

Aaron about my dream, my missing father and my theory that somehow the dream and his disappearance were related.

Aaron listened carefully before he spoke, "Interpreting dreams is not my gift, but I know of someone who has the gift, his name is "Mari". Would you like to meet him and tell him your dream? He may be able to tell you what it means."

"Yes, I'd like that very much."

Aaron communicated with his sphere and it left to deliver the message to the other spheres. The way Aaron explained it, the spheres would pass the message along and in the blink of an eye the message would be delivered to Mari's sphere and ask him to come over.

"It just so happens that the Junior Council is in town. Whenever the Supreme Council meets, they bring their eldest child with them. The children get together to discuss the issues relating to young people and then they pass their findings on to the adults on the Supreme Council. Mari is the leader of the Junior Council and he has the gift of interpreting dreams. I have asked him to come and join us."

While we waited, Aaron left the room and returned with two translation devices. He handed each one of us a device and then showed us how to operate them.

A few minutes later there was a chime indicating a new arrival. Aaron stood and walked to the door. He touched the right spot on the wall and watched as the door slid open with a quiet hiss. Four slightly younger and smaller versions of the adults entered the room.

I felt my heart race as I looked into the beautiful eyes of the one who stepped forward to greet me first.

"My name is Mari," he said, "I am the leader of the Junior Council and this is Makai, Anaiya and then Maliyah."

They had been told that hand shaking was the traditional Earth greeting. When Mari extended his hand, I took it and just as we touched, I felt a jolt of electricity. The electric shock was much like the static shock you get when you drag your feet on carpet and then touch a door knob...

(ZAP!)

Except this shock came with much, much more intensity. I felt almost... light-headed.

(What is happening to me?)

Each one of them stepped forward to shake our hands. They all seemed to be very excited to meet us. But there was no shock when I touched them.

(That was weird.)

Aaron invited the new arrivals to sit in the main room. I watched them, I couldn't help but smile. They were roughly my age and more importantly they were roughly my height. On Earth I was taller than most kids and as tall as many adults, but on 'Pardes' I was normal.

(I would never be a freak here.)

Although people on 'Pardes' lived for thousands of years, that longevity thing didn't kick in until puberty.

(Which I thought was completely unfair, they were on fast forward through the best part only to spend thousands of years as grown-ups.)

We all took a seat in Aaron's main room and I relayed my dream once again. The one who called himself Mari was the first to speak.

"I think that you're correct in your interpretation, however your dream has two meanings. I believe that the man you saw on the hill was a representation of your heavenly father and that's why his face was obscured. I believe that the hill you are standing on represents your dying planet and the hill the Lord was standing on represents 'Pardes'. I believe that the Lord was preparing you to come here and help us. I think that the man also represents your earthly father and the Lord was preparing you for something but what that 'something' is I don't know."

I looked around the room and I could see that each of them were in agreement.

We talked for a while longer before it was time for Mari and the rest of the Junior Council members to go. First Aaron showed the visitors to the door and then he showed us to the guest room.

The guest room had two beds which were obviously designed for someone over seven feet tall and it seemed to swallow us up. But the odd size wasn't enough to keep us awake, and it didn't take long for us to drift off to sleep, I was exhausted.

***

There was a knock at the door later that night that startled me awake. I couldn't hear the conversation but the tone didn't sound friendly. I shook Bella awake and we slipped into our clothes. Then I went to the bedroom door and listened to the raised voices coming from the main room.

"My name is Gimel. My associates and I have come to see the Alien children you are sheltering. We want to inquire as to their intentions."

"At this hour of the night," Aaron asked.

"Lucifer says they are to testify at the hearing."

There was a pause and Aaron must have looked surprised because Gimel said, "Don't look so surprised Aaron, yes we know who they are and why they are here and we have come for them. We are not going to allow them to stand in the way of us becoming Gods."

I started looking around the room and said, "We need to hide!"

"The balcony," Bella said as she raced towards it.

I knew that the intruders would reach Aaron's room first so we should have enough time to find a good hiding place.

We made it out onto the balcony just as the intruders entered Aaron's room and began searching. We were more than a mile above the ground. The nightly wind that blew the rain clouds in and out were brutal. We ducked down below the rail when we saw the intruders in

Aaron's room, tearing it apart, looking for us. I peeked over the top of the rail in time to see the intruders on Aaron's balcony and I knew the guest bedroom and balcony would be the next to be searched.

(We need to find a place to hide... fast!)

We had just one problem. The guest room balcony, like the rest of the planet was disgustingly clutter free. There was nowhere to hide.

"What is it with these people?" Bella shouted in frustration as the wind howled around us.

"We have to get off this balcony." I shouted, Bella nodded in agreement.

Keeping to the shadows, I climbed out onto the ledge that connected the two balconies, Bella was right behind me.

We stood on the ledge and held onto a decorative protrusion just above our heads. The howling wind was deafening, the buffeting felt like body blows.

My heart raced as we slid along.

I didn't dare lift my feet and risk losing my balance. I looked back at Bella, she looked like she was as afraid as I was. She also seemed just as determined.

The words

Don't look down

were echoing in my head.

The buildings crystalline surface was smooth and slippery which made the footing treacherous but we kept moving, slowly sliding along the two foot ledge. Just before I reached the other side a gust of wind caused me to loose my balance.

I slipped.

I lost my grip on the decorative protrusion and suddenly my feet slid out from under me on the wet crystalline ledge. I felt myself desperately clutching for the balcony... anything, to keep from falling.

I heard Bella scream my name over the howl of the wind.

(Oh God, help me!)

At the last minute I was able to grab onto the balcony railing. Somehow I managed to hold on. I felt Bella's hands grab my shirt and pull me up. She had somehow moved past me and was now on Aaron's balcony. I managed to get my leg over the rail and fling my body up and over, onto the balcony. I hit the ground hard. Bella tumbled down on top of me just as one of the intruders stepped out onto the guest bedroom balcony and looked around.

I scrambled to my feet and peeked over the rail. I tried to watch them, I had to see what they would do next, but the wind was strong.

(Yeah, like blow my eyeballs right out of their socket strong.)

I caught a glimpse of them standing on the balcony before I had to pinch my eyes shut.

The howling wind was deafening and just as it began to subside, it carried their words over to me.

"They are not here, he must have hidden them somewhere, take him instead," the leader Gimel said before he lead the group inside.

I could hear the sound of a scuffle.

(Oh No, Oh no!)

I raced into the main room but no one was there. I caught a glimpse of them as they left the apartment. They were all wearing black cloth frocks with hoods.

I heard Bella come up behind me.

"Aaron is Gone, Lucifer's goons took him," I told her.

***

SECTION #13

That night they kidnapped Aaron...

I couldn't believe it. I hadn't anticipated that they would do such a thing, because it didn't make sense to. I would have never left him alone with them. They had no idea what they were doing, which made them unpredictable, which made them dangerous.

Chapter 19

I RAN TO the door and frantically tried to locate the spot that opened it. By the time I stumbled upon the right spot, they were already in the elevator and the elevator door was closing. We sprinted down the hall and caught the next car down.

The streets were empty and quiet, the rains had come and gone but the walkway was still wet.

"They can't be far," I said, "they would normally use the "HTD" to get them to where they needed to go, but somehow I don't believe that option is available to them."

There was no detectable movement, so we stood still while we listened. I could hear the hurried splashes of retreating footfalls coming from a near-by alley. We ran down the crystal walkway towards the sounds in pursuit of what we hoped were the robed intruders who had taken Aaron.

We soon reached a point where the sounds of the men fleeing went into two different directions.

"We need to split up," I said, Bella agreed. So Bella followed the sounds in one direction while I followed the sounds that went in the other.

I was starting to get worried. The sounds I was following were fading in and out as they bounced off the buildings. And then they suddenly stopped. I stood there for a minute trying to pick up the sounds again but it was no use, there was nothing. Then I thought I saw something in the alley, a man was standing near the next intersection. The ambient light made him almost ghostly in appearance. I cautiously moved towards him... he was still a few feet away when he called to me by name.

(He called my name! How did he know my name?)

***

Chapter 20

MUST BE ONE of Lucifer's goons. Can't say I was surprised, I was expecting Lucifer to send one of them to stop me.

(Fine with me.)

I was angry and hurt and I was afraid for Aaron... somebody needed to pay... why not make one of Lucifer's goons the first?

I approached him cautiously, I didn't want him to run away before I could get my hands on him.

(Yeah, just a couple more steps... just wait right there, buddy... you have no idea what is about to happen to you, do you?)

... and when I was close enough... I realized... I knew this man, it was one of the Junior Council members, it was Mari.

"Mari, what are you doing here?"

"I was about to ask you the same thing," Mari said.

"I am looking for a group of men in black hooded frocks."

"I saw them running down that alley," he said pointing.

"But how, why?"

"I was home sleeping and the lord woke me up. He told me to come to this intersection and wait for you. And that I should 'show you the way'. I thought he meant spiritually but, now I know He meant it literally."

I smiled, jumped into his arms and kissed him on the cheek, then I turned and ran away.

Mari called after me, "What's going on?"

I sprinted down the alley and shouted over my shoulder, "I'll explain it to you later," just before I disappeared into the darkness.

At each intersection I met a different member of the Junior Council... Makai, Anaiya and then Maliyah. Each had the same story, they were home asleep and the Lord came to them. He asked them to go to a specific location, wait for me to come by and to "show her the way".

I was close and closing in. I heard hurried footsteps just ahead. I slowed to a trot to better get a bearing on the sounds echoing off the crystal buildings. I turned a corner and found them.

There were five of them with Aaron between them. The men carried no weapons, Aaron was not bound. They were guiding him, he resisted a little but not much, not the way a kidnap victim on Earth would resist.

(These people were so innocent, even the bad guys were polite.)

As soon as I caught up with them, they all stopped. They were surprised to see me.

(You know that feeling you get when you are watching a scary movie and you just KNOW something bad is about to happen. You get goose bumps... you can feel your hair standing up... yeah, that's the feeling I was getting now.)

There was someone else in the alley...

...someone who was keeping to the shadows.

"I know you," a voice came from behind me. I looked around to see that same "movie star" handsome man who had been back on Earth, looking up at my window.

He stepped from the shadows into the light.

"Lucifer!" Aaron's shouted recognition echoed throughout the alley. I turned and found myself face to face with the Devil himself.

"I know you," Lucifer repeated as he pulled his hood back, "and I know your father."

"What do you know about my father?"

Lucifer slowly circled me and said, "I know that he is missing and I also know where he is, I can take you to him. All you need to do is walk away. This is none of your business."

Don't listen to him,

the small still voice said.

I faced Lucifer, "If you really know me, then you know that your goons are no match for me. Now, are you going to tell them to let Aaron go or shall I."

Lucifer stopped and stared at me for what seemed like forever. Then with a dismissive wave of his hand Lucifer said, "Let him go, we don't need him anymore. We have a more valuable hostage. Your best friend Bella. If you show up tomorrow you will never see her again."

I was shaken but I recovered, I prayed silently and while I prayed I could see Lucifer's expression change from arrogant triumph into something different, something I recognized as fear.

Resist the devil, and he will flee from you.

I took a step towards him and spoke quietly so that only he could hear.

"I can see that you are afraid and I know that it's not me you're afraid of. But you are afraid of my heavenly father." I paused and looked him in the eye. "You mentioned earlier that you know me, well... I know you too. Now I see you for what you really are. I understand that the only power you hold over me is the power I give you. I used to be afraid of you, I'm not afraid of you anymore and I won't listen to your lies. In the name of Jesus, get behind me Satan."

A flash of red hot anger washed across his face, but he did not linger. He turned and ran away leaving his goons standing in the alley... confused and alone.

I watched the Devil flee for a moment before I turned to face the goons.

"I hope you guys are good lawyers, because you stink at kidnapping."

I took a couple of steps towards them. I wasn't sure what I was about to do... I was angry and I hadn't thought that far ahead.

"You're gonna have to do better than this if you want to keep playing on this side of the fence."

I paused and stared them down. Aaron stepped away from them, his head was on a swivel. He was dividing his attention between watching me and then the way the goons reacted to me.

"Now... Aaron tells me that the people of this world have no concept of good and evil, which means you have no concept of violence."

The goons watched me warily; they didn't know what to do so they just stood there. I took a step closer.

""I come from the toughest part of the toughest city on a fallen world. What made you think that you were a match for me anyway?"

They listened to my words, I could almost see the little wheels turning in their heads. They were considering all of the obvious factors.

They outnumbered me five to one.

They had a substantial size advantage, I was almost a foot shorter.

They were grown men, I was twelve .

I took another step, making a show of rolling up my sleeves.

I said, "I know Lucifer has probably filled your head with all sorts of things. But now that he has run away from a twelve year old girl. Do you think it's possible that Lucifer has lied to you?"

The goons were getting nervous. It wasn't lost on them that I had apparently just frightened away the man who claimed to be the one true GOD.

"So you want to eat the Forbidden Fruit and learn all about good and evil? Well... you already know about the good, because you live in paradise."

I took a couple more steps.

"Why don't I introduce you to the other side of that coin... we can start tonight. How about I show you what a Los Angeles style butt kicking feels like?"

They weren't at all sure what a "butt kicking" was, but they were sure they didn't want to find out. They backed away a few steps and then turned to run. I watched the alley where they had disappeared for a few minutes before I turned back to Aaron.

"Are you OK?"

Aaron nodded.

"Let's get you to a safe place," I told Aaron after I was sure the goons were gone.

"But what about Bella?"

"First things first."

"This is unsettling, this whole world is a safe place, at least it used to be."

"And it will be again, but not tonight."

"Their aggressive attitude is unheard of."

"Lucifer is getting desperate. He is seeing his plan fall apart before his eyes. I can't leave you alone; I'll leave you with the Junior Council. Satan won't attack the children of the council members the day before the hearing."

I retraced my steps, collecting the Junior Council members along the way. When Aaron was away safely with them, I set out to find Bella.

***

SECTION #14

Satan was desperate to stop me from testifying. He failed in his attempt to abduct us, so he tried to kidnap Aaron. That didn't work either. But now Bella was missing and if I were to believe Satan ...

(Yeah right, he's trustworthy)

...then I would never see Bella again.

I searched until the sun started to illuminate the night time sky. The streets were just beginning to fill with people and it would soon be impossible to spot her in this land of giants.

Just when it appeared hopeless...

I spotted Bella walking towards me!

She had escaped!

***

Chapter 21

"Bella!" I shouted. We met on the sidewalk and embraced. We were both crying our eyes out.

"I confronted Satan last night, he told me they captured you and that I would never see you again if I testified."

"Well, surprise surprise, the devil lied," Bella said. "Actually he only half lied, I allowed them to capture me because I thought they would take me to Aaron. But it became obvious that they were just trying to keep me away from the hearing. When I figured they weren't the ones who had him, I escaped."

"How did you manage that?"

Bella allowed a sly smile creep across her face.

"I remembered what you said about them all being vain and selfish politicians, so I told them I wanted them all to give speeches before the council today and when they were practicing, I simply walked away. They aren't very smart."

"It's not that they are dumb, Bella. It's just that they haven't had thousands of years in a fallen state to master trickery and deceit," I pointed out.

Bella laughed. "Well I guess good help is hard to find when you are trying to spread evil on a perfect planet. It must be driving ole Beelzebub crazy."

"Ain't that the truth," I said, unable to hide the laughter in my voice.

Then I thought about the hearing as I looked up at the brightening sky. I remembered that the hearing was to start at dawn, we were running out of time.

***

Chapter 22

"**The devil may** win this time," I said, "We won't make it back in time for the hearing."

"At least Aaron will be there," Bella said, "the bad guys weren't able to get him far enough away from the "Great Hall" on foot because there is no transportation and obviously the Lord was not going to help them escape."

"What did you say?"

"I said at least Aaron will be there."

"No, no, after that."

"I said at least the Lord didn't help them get away."

"That's it! Bella remember how we got to the city so quickly. Aaron said all we had to do was have faith and start on a journey and the Lord would do the rest. Maybe it will work for us. We may not have one of those fancy spheres, but we are still children of GOD."

"It's worth a try, but let's pray first," Bella said.

So that's what we did, right there on the walkway, we closed our eyes, knelt and prayed. When we opened our eyes we were surprised to see that people on the street had stopped and extended their hands and started praying with us without even knowing what we were praying for.

We stood and started walking with our destination in mind and just like before, in the blink of an eye we arrived at the "Great Hall".

***

"They are ready for you," the Guardian announced as he swung open the doors. He led us down the corridor to the floor of the Great Hall. I saw a small platform with a podium in the center. The three plaintiffs were seated on the platform along with their attorney. I recognized one of them from last night, he was one of the goons that attempted to kidnap Aaron. On the right side of the platform Aaron waited, he smiled broadly when he saw us.

While the planetary judges settled into their seats. Aaron explained what would happen next.

"Since you weren't born here you don't have a sphere. We communicate with our minds but you will have to communicate the old-fashioned way, with your mouth. Your ear piece translators stopped working sometime last night. Your words will instead be picked up, translated and transmitted to that large black box you see on the wall over there. The black box will then broadcast your words to each of spheres in the dome. Those spheres will in turn relay the audio along with the video to every sphere everywhere, so the whole world will be watching and listening."

I was listening to Aaron's words... trying not to be overwhelmed by the enormity of it all. I watched the judges as they settled in. I looked up at the millions of spheres that swarmed overhead.

I had already started to pray for the right words. I stepped to the podium and the room fell silent. I opened my mouth and the words just seemed to tumble out.

"I come from a planet that was at one time much like yours. In our world we have a Bible which is a collection of writings, poems, songs and letters inspired by God. It contains the answers to the deep-est needs of a fallen humanity. It is meant to shed light where there is darkness.

"The first book in our Bible is called Genesis. In the second chapter it describes how God created our Garden of Eden. Within it he placed animals and trees that bore fruit and in the center of the garden the Lord placed two trees, just like the ones you have here.

My ancestors were given free will just as you have been. We were given the same admonishment not to eat of 'the Tree of Life' nor 'the Tree of the Knowledge of Good and Evil' that you were."

I went on to talk about the fall of man, how sin entered the world. Next I spoke of the Christ, his death and resurrection. I spoke of the Holy Spirit and the future triumphant return of Jesus Christ himself.

"The bible tells us that Jesus, the Lord Jesus Christ himself will descend from Heaven with a shout with the voice of the Archangel and the trumpet of God. And the dead in Christ will rise first and we who are alive and remain shall be caught up together in the air and so shall we forever be with the lord.

"Don't you see... On my planet, in our fallen state, we dream of someday having what you have everyday... experiencing what you take for granted."

Finally I spoke about the state of the planet Earth today. How life on my fallen planet compared to life on this planet where the fall never occurred.

I spoke for what must have been hours, supported and strength-ened by the Holy Spirit. When I finished a recess was ordered by the Presiding Judge.

"The good news is we believe you. People on our planet can't hide their true feelings. It's reflected in our eyes and our robes which are tuned to match our moods. Just like the spheres, blue and green are colors for positive emotions while red and orange are the colors of anger or distrust. Look, all of the judges are green," Aaron said.

I was suddenly exhausted, I nodded then I collapsed into my chair.

***

The recess ended the judges returned and took their assigned places.

Before the proceedings resumed Aaron walked over to me. He activated his personal translator and said, "I have to apologize, the 'black box' has stopped working. And I have to turn this one off because it interferes with the spheres." He was about to explain when one of the Guardians walked up and interrupted him with a tap on the shoulder. After a short conversation he turned his attention back to me and explained, "We haven't used this equipment in a thousand or so years. There are still a couple of technicians alive who are familiar with this equipment and I've just been told they are on their way."

I acknowledged Aaron and took a moment to look around the gallery. I saw Lucifer enter the arena and take a seat, I could tell that he was not too pleased to see either of us. I got Bella's attention and pointed Lucifer out.

"That's Lucifer. It took him a few thousand years, but he finally found someone both narcissistic and gullible enough to champion his cause."

***

The presiding judge called the Council to order. Next he signaled Aaron to make his presentation.

Aaron presented his case for about 30 minutes and by the time he finished; the colors reflected around the room were entirely blue and green. He returned to his seat and turned on his personal translator.

"So that's it then," I asked Aaron when he took his seat.

"No," Aaron said, "now the lawyers take over."

When the plaintiffs' lawyer began his presentation he was not received well, almost all of the Judges' robes were red.

We could only watch as the lawyer for the plaintiffs presented his case. Out of the corner of my eye I caught sight of a strange looking little man in an ill fitting robe. He approached the 'black box'. He tinkered with it for a moment and then gave us a "thumbs up". The little man flashed a broad smile and I heard him say in perfect English, "Your equipment is working now."

We had missed all of Aaron's and most of the lawyer's arguments because of the equipment failure. But we were able to tune in just as the plaintiffs' lawyer was wrapping up.

"... and where is he, where is the Lord? How is it possible that the Lord God Almighty has time to stroll through the garden with every living person, but he is not here to defend himself," the lawyer was saying.

"Objection!" Aaron jumped to his feet, his eyes and robe flashing fiery red. "You all know the answer to that, he is God. His word is law, it's not a 'position' to be debated or defended. It's the way things are! We have free will and he cannot interfere with our free will. The Counselor is out of order with those arguments by the rules established by this body."

"My apologies," the plaintiffs' attorney continued dripping with fake humility, "but that goes to the very heart of the case. It is my clients' position that the Lord is not so all powerful as he would have you believe. Our position is that the source of his power is the so-called forbidden fruit. Our suit alleges that God himself ate of the tree and now seeks to deny us all the same knowledge that has made him what he is today... He isn't Almighty at all; he just got to the tree first."

The lawyer finished with a flurry and a murmur rose among the judges. It was obvious the lawyer's arguments were persuasive because their emotions were visible in their eyes and reflected in their robes. The sea of red had almost turned completely to green.

The lawyer winked at Lucifer as he strutted back to his seat and for the first time since the hearing was announced, it appeared as if they might actually pull it off.

***

Chapter 23

"Lawyers," Bella said in disgust, "I always knew that they were from another planet."

She was saying something else, but I didn't hear her because I was already on my feet heading for the podium.

"This is stupid!" My voice echoed throughout the chamber. "I am from a world where that man over there," I pointed an angry finger at Lucifer, "convinced someone to eat the Forbidden Fruit. The people of my world would give almost anything to have what you have here... to go back to the way it was. You have no idea what you are giving up." My impassioned plea was having some effect as the judges robes began to change.

"I object!" The plaintiffs' lawyer jumped to his feet and charged the podium. "She had her say. Besides there has been no offer of proof that she is indeed from another world and even if she was, there is no proof that any of the conditions she has described exists. It's my clients' position that this is a trick concocted to sway this body."

I felt my frustration level rising, I didn't come this far to fail. But all I could do was watch helplessly as the plaintiffs' lawyer hammered his point home. When he finished he winked triumphantly at Lucifer and Lucifer grinned his acknowledgement.

(I had to admit the lawyer was right, there wasn't proof.
So, what if...)

"I have a simple solution," I said with sudden insight, "the lawyer's argument is correct... all you have is my word. If the issue here is proof that what I say is true, the plaintiffs are welcome to come back with me. That way they can reap all the rewards such knowledge has to offer. That way they can learn from those who have had the knowledge for thousands of years."

A clamor arose amongst the judges. There was a visible wave of agreement sweeping the room. I noticed the cocky smile drop from Lucifer's confident face. But just as quickly it returned, lest anyone know he hated the idea.

Aaron noticed it too.

"It must be a good idea if Lucifer is against it," Aaron whispered into my ear. Then Aaron closed his eyes and consulted with the Father in prayer.

The three plaintiffs were looking at each other nodding enthusiastically. The prospect of possessing god-like powers intoxicated them and after all of these years, suddenly it was within their grasp. Even their lawyer liked the idea.

Aaron finished his prayers and called for quiet. When the chamber was silent he approached the podium.

"I have just been in consultation with our Father. He told me that if you travel to Earth, you will indeed possess the knowledge of good and evil."

What had been a low clamor threatened to explode into a roar. The presiding judge pounded his gavel and called for quiet.

Aaron continued, "...and as a consequence of possessing that knowledge, you may never return to this garden."

The plaintiffs' lawyer jumped to his feet again. "But if they can never return how can they report back to this body in order for the judges to make their decision?"

I rose and again addressed the judges.

"My technology is capable of sending objects across space-time. I suggest that after the plaintiffs experience the advantages and drawbacks that come with this great knowledge, they be allowed to use their spheres to send a simple message back to this world.

"Eat" or "Don't Eat" and for anyone who is considering coming to Earth in the future, I suggest the plaintiffs also send a message advising "Come" or "Don't Come". It will take me about a week to build the transport devices that will send the spheres back to Pardes. I suggest you reconvene back here seven days from our departure to receive their recommendations."

***

SECTION #15

So I testified and now it was time to go home. But we would not be alone. The plan was for three of them to come back with us on a "fact finding" mission.

(Whatever)

They were calling the three who were about to travel to Earth "Explorers" like they were Lindbergh or Armstrong or something. I had a different name for them but it wasn't polite so I kept it to myself.

The planet's scientists estimated that it would take about three days to build and test the devices to send Bella, me and the three "explorers" to Earth.

Bella and I decided to spend those three days praying and in fellowship with the members of the Junior Supreme Council.

✳✳✳

Chapter 24

MAKAI, ANAIYA AND Maliyah spent a lot of time with Bella. They were warned not to be too curious about Earth. They already knew a lot because of my testimony. But there was a tipping point where they could conceivably learn too much and be kicked out of the Garden and no one wanted to risk it. Most of the conversation centered on Bella's curiosity about what it was like to literally walk with God and to live in the Garden of Eden.

Mari and I also spent a lot of time together.

***

"Everything is so green here. It's beautiful," I said. "I still can't get over how blue your sky is."

"If you think this is beautiful, you should see our ocean… the water is bluer than the sky."

"Can you take me there?"

"Sure, If you want, I can take you now."

"I want." I looked over at Bella. She was with the other Junior Council members. They were sitting in a circle completely immersed in Bella's favorite activity... eating. There was a pile of wafers in the middle and Bella was busy corrupting their minds and bodies with junk food.

"We're going to the Ocean," I said.

Bella looked around with what could best be described as a, "What are you talking about and why are you bothering me," look on her face.

(How Rude!)

"Do you want to come?" I asked, ignoring her, "are you still here" look.

"Heck no, the ocean is filled with… all of those creatures!"

"You mean fish," I said.

"Yeah," she said with a shiver, "… and water!"

"No… duh!"

"Whatever…" she said rolling her eyes. "Water is wet! And you know full well what salt water does to my hair… and yours too!"

(Unbelievable!)

Before I could respond Anaiya's sphere, shot between us and almost playfully bumped Mari's sphere. Both sphere's then spun around one another before shooting straight up and out of sight for a few seconds. When the spheres returned, they both flashed blue and then a weird pink color, I had never seen before. The spheres separated and Anaiya's sphere floated back to the circle and after a few seconds of communicating with the sphere's belonging to the other council members and then the council members themselves, the Jr. Council members laughed.

"Come on, let's go," Mari said.

"Why did your sphere turn pink, why are they laughing?"

"Bella is showing them the different foods of your world," Mari said as his eyes and robe turned the same color pink as his sphere.

I could tell he wasn't telling me everything.

(He's embarrassed, pink must be the color of embarrassment.)

I shot Bella a look but before I could say something, Mari was pulling me away. We set out together for the ocean. We took the HTD and as always it took no time for us to get there.

I knew my eyes must have widened three times their normal size and I know my mouth had dropped open. Fine white sand, as white as newly fallen snow seemed to swirl around a gigantic black rock that was just up ahead.

Before long we were standing on the rock, it seemed to float over the water. I nervously looked down, the water was a clear crisp blue. It was so clean, I could see the bottom which was at least fifty feet down. I watched as various sea creatures swam below us. Some of them I recognized, like giant turtles and dolphins, but there were so many I had never seen before.

"Do you like it?" Mari asked looking deep into my eyes, into my soul.

(What is happening here?)

I nodded yes, unable to speak.

"Let me show you something." He grabbed onto my hand and just like before, there was that shock of electricity.

"Ouch what is that?" I asked pulling my hand back.

"So, you felt it too?" He asked, his eyes were wide with excitement. He smiled warmly.

"Of course I did, but you are the only one that shocks me... how come?"

Mari didn't answer, he just stood there with a dopey smile on his face. "Follow me, there is something I want to show you." We walked for a few minutes then Mari stopped. There were about a dozen small bungalow style cottages just ahead. My family has a beach house just over there," he said, pointing at a small purple and green cottage. We should have a swim suit there that will fit you."

"Swim suit?"

"Sure, unless they swim in their clothes on your world."

"Swim? What… where!"

"It's a surprise," was all he said before he turned and jogged to the house.

Swim suits on this planet, like everything else were… perfect. One size truly did "fit all". As soon as I slipped into it, the suit conformed to my body like one of those high-tech wet-suits. Before long I was changed and on my way outside. Mari was waiting for me on the beach.

Mari was wearing a similar suit.

"I'm surprised, I guess I expected you to swim in your magic robe."

Mari rolled his eyes, just one of the bad habits he has picked up from Bella, then he laughed.

"See that huge rock about 100 feet off-shore?"

"Yes."

"That's where we are swimming to."

"Okay." I said as I took off my sandals and flung them on the sand. The white sand here was like millions of tiny, fluffy white marshmallows between your toes.

"The sand feels weird," I giggled as I stood up.

"What does it feel like on your planet?"

"It's coarse, kinda like a million tiny pieces of sharp rocks beneath your feet."

Mari smiled. "Come on," he said. We walked to the water just as a wave broke against the shore. I prepared myself for the cold icy blue water… so I thought. But when the water reached us, it wasn't cold at all.

"Oh my gosh. Your world is so different from everything I have grown to expect. I don't think I will ever get used to it."

"Get used to what?"

"Everything here."

Mari laughed again and said, "You haven't even seen the best part… come on." Mari said as he half dragged me into the water. When we were deep enough to swim he let me go and began swimming towards the large rock. It looked more like the top of a mountain as we got closer, with the majority of it under water.

We reached the rock and Mari stopped and waited for me. A few seconds later we were treading water, facing each other.

"OK... Now what?" I said.

Then without a word, just a wink... Mari dove beneath the surface. Now I considered myself an excellent swimmer but I had a hard time keeping up with Mari. We dove deeper and deeper, I was starting to get scared, my lungs were starting to burn. I caught a glimpse of Mari entering the mouth of a small narrow cave at the base of the mountain. It was dark, but there was a light at the end.

I made it through the cave and started up. I mercifully broke the surface before my chest exploded. I took in a long sweet breath. I looked around. I was in an underwater cavern. There was a white sandy beach just ten feet away, I headed for it. When I came out of the water, I saw Mari, standing on the beach, waiting for me. He took my hand and helped me to my feet. There was just enough light to see. The cavern was beautiful, like a natural cathedral of blue and green crystal.

We walked through the cavern until we came to a group of large rocks arranged in a ring.

"When I was little my family and I would spend weekends at this beach. But this cavern is a special place."

He paused for a minute and looked around.

"When my parents were children they would race to that rock. They discovered this cavern. They would come here and talk for hours. It is here, in this cavern, they realized that they were partners for life." He grew silent again and started to play with his fingers. We sat there in silence for what felt like forever.

"How do you know who you are suppose to be with for the rest of your life on your planet?" He finally said.

"You don't really. You meet, you date... if you can stand each other you decide you are in love and then you get married. To tell you the truth people claim to be in love, get married and then sometimes stay together. But more often than not, they break up." Mari listened and nodded his head.

I looked into his eyes and asked, "How do you tell on your planet?" He held up his hand…"By this," he finally said.

"Your hand? Does it start glowing or something?"

"No." He laughed at me. "God has created for each of us, our perfect mate. That shock that we felt, the one between you and me, that is how we tell who we will spend the rest of our lives with. There is only one person who can cause such a reaction. We spend our whole lives wondering about our perfect mate. By the time we reach our teens, we become aware of that person, but we don't know who or where they are. It takes about seven years but eventually we are drawn together. No knows how, no one can explain it, we stopped trying."

***

Chapter 25

"But we can't." I frowned, tears were starting to well up in my eyes. "This can't be right, it must be some kind of mistake.

"God doesn't make mistakes."

"But I come from another world, fifty light years away!"

"And yet you are here," he said softly as he took my hand into his.

I felt my head starting to spin. I changed the subject.

"Where is your sphere?" I asked looking around.

"On the beach."

"Why isn't it with you?"

"Because this is a special place, a secret place. A place where I can be alone and think and pray and be with the Lord... not have the sphere reading my thoughts.. have anyone else thinking with me or trying to find out what I think. And since the spheres can't swim, this is the only place where I can be alone."

"What do you think about when you are here?"

"You I guess," he said looking into my eyes.

My mouth dropped open.

"But you have only known me for a few days."

"I wasn't thinking about you in particular, I was thinking about what my future partner would be like."

"And now that you have met me what do you think about?"

"About this," he said. He leaned over towards me and before I knew it, our lips were touching. The kiss was sweet, simple and filled with love. I pulled away.

"Mari, we..."

"I know," he cut me off. "But we did."

"We should go back the others will worry about us," I said standing up. And before I had time to stop myself, I walked back to the shore and dove into the water. Mari followed close behind. When we reached the beach, I found my shoes and ran back to the cabin to change. We didn't take the HTD home. We walked most of the way in silence.

"Michelle," Mari called out my name softly, I looked at him.

"I'm not sorry I did that," he said with a shrug of his shoulder.

"Neither am I," I said with a nervous smile before I had to look away.

***

Over the next couple of days we were careful not to be alone together. But the heaviness in my heart seemed to grow with each passing day.

***

"Hey, there you are," Mari said cheerfully as he stepped onto the balcony of Aaron's home. I turned to face him with a weak smile.

"Hey," I replied and then turned back to take in what probably would be my last sunset in paradise. "We leave tomorrow," I choked out.

"I know you both are 'supposed' to leave tomorrow," he said cheerfully. I turned and faced him, surprise flashed across my face.

"What do you mean?"

"I've been thinking and praying... so has the other Junior Council members and we all have come to the same conclusion."

"Which is?"

"You should petition to stay here."

I smiled back at him and hugged him tightly, but that small still voice spoke to me now.

You have to go back, you don't belong here.

When we released my smile was gone and when Mari saw my face, he knew... and his smile slowly faded away.

"Mari, I..."

"I know, you can't."

"We can't leave my mom, we are all she has," I heard my voice say and with every word that poured from my mouth, I became more confident that this was what I would do.

Mari's eyes were a soft purple a color that I had never seen before.

"Your eyes," I said.

"Now I know what you meant when you talked about heart ache, cause I feel it now."

A small smile tugged at the corner of my lips at Mari's use of the word 'cause'. It was nice knowing that at least something of our presence had rubbed off on the "Junior Council" even if it only was our bad grammar. But who was I kidding, I would be leaving behind much more than bad grammar. It would be difficult for both of us. We both knew that we could become good friends and according to Mari, "Partners for Life," but soon I would be fifty light years away and we would never see each other again.

There was so much of his world he wanted to show me and who wouldn't want to stay in paradise.

(For the first time in my life, I don't feel like a freak.)

I can't lie, I was tempted, but then I thought about my mom at home all alone. I thought about what Lucifer had said. He claimed he knew where my dad was... He claimed to be able to take me to him. That meant that he was still alive... didn't it?

I have plans for you, You have to go back.

(I have to go back.)

***

Chapter 26

True to their word, three days after being given the order, the scientists finished building the special single use transporter.

On the appointed day after all the good-byes were said, the three "travelers" stood with us on the floor of the Great Hall, waiting to be transported to the planet they all now knew as Earth.

To everyone's surprise their attorney had petitioned and obtained permission to accompany his clients. Aaron stood solemnly behind me as I watched the group and waited to depart. Aaron followed my eyes to the grinning lawyer.

"The good news is that he is one of the last lawyers on the planet and as of last night most of Lucifer's followers have left the school," Aaron said. "There is not much use for lawyers here," Aaron continued, "But sooner or later Lucifer will persuade someone to attend his tiny law school."

"Speak of the devil," Bella said as she watched Lucifer make his entrance into the hall. Lucifer made a show of congratulating each of the four travelers. He approached them one by one, shaking their hands while slapping them on the back.

"He's acting as if they are going on a great and wonderful adventure, knowing full well what awaits them on Earth," Bella observed. We both watched the spectacle and it sickened us.

Bella said, "Now they are grinning and patting Lucifer on the back. They won't feel the same way about him about an hour from now, will they?"

"Well they heard the truth, but decided to listen to Lucifer instead.

They will soon have their reward," I said thoughtfully. "We will help them out as much as possible, help them settle in, find a church if they are interested."

"They are going to need jobs; minimum wage is about all they will be qualified for. It's not going to be easy for them, not by a long shot. Not after a lifetime in paradise," Bella said shaking her head.

We both fell quiet while we looked around the hall expectantly. As if reading our minds Aaron interrupted our thoughts.

"He's not here," Aaron said regretfully.

"We are not going to see him before we go are we?" Bella asked.

"No," Aaron answered with a shake of his head, "I'm afraid not. The Lord said that in your fallen state, for you to look upon him would mean death and he still has work for you on your planet."

"I would have liked to have seen him face-to-face," I said unable to hide my disappointment. "I have so many questions for him."

"To everything there is a season," he told me to tell you, "it's not your time yet."

I nodded and then looked up and watched as millions of spheres again filled the dome of the Great Hall. They shone bright blue and green much brighter now than they had been before.

"The whole world has turned out to see you off," Aaron observed.

"Why are the lights so bright?"

"Just as the color is an indication of emotion, the brightness is an indication of the intensity of the emotion." Aaron said.

We watched as the intense light reflected throughout the Crystal city until it appeared the entire planet was awash with the blue and green.

***

It was time to leave Pardes. The teleportation device rose up in the air just above our heads and began its now familiar vibrating and beeping as it warmed up. The six of us stood still and waited to be hurled across the galaxy to Earth.

Children were not allowed in the Great Hall, Bella and I being the exception, so our new friends were not there to see us off.

I looked up at all of the spheres swarming high above my head and wondered which one of them belonged to Mari. Then I saw it... a single sphere, all by itself, hovering just above the platform. It was that same soft purple I had seen in his eyes last night. It moved much slower than the other spheres, as if it was trying to process feelings and emotions that it had never had to process before. And that attempt to process those emotions was sapping away most of its energy, effecting its ability to fly.

"Goodbye Mari," I told the sphere as it struggled to gain altitude and join the others.

My eyes fell on Aaron.

"Goodbye Aaron, I will look you up when I get to Heaven," I promised.

"Goodbye Michelle, goodbye Bella, thank you. I will never forget you," he said. The judges stood and began applauding. Then in an instant, the applause faded and Pardes disappeared.

***

Chapter 27

WE MATERIALIZED IN the driveway of my Los Angeles home. The traveler's eyes went wide at the sight of the urban sprawl which had replaced their beautiful garden.

Their elation vanished when the polluted air attacked their eyes and lungs. They watched in horror as their beautiful robes dissolved in the comparatively toxic air. They stood there ashamed at their near nakedness as their undergarments also began to dissolve. Their once colorful eyes were now a dull black. With each breath their skin began to loose its bright orange luster, turning a kinda jaundiced pale and lifeless color.

"Welcome to Los Angeles ladies and gentlemen."

(Yeah Los Angeles, The City of Angels.)

That stuff burning your lungs is called smog. It will take a while but you'll get used to it," I told them.

They didn't hear me because they all had dropped to their knees coughing and wheezing. One by one, as the realization hit them, they looked up at me and although they could not speak, their red watering eyes said it all.

"He lied to us!"

"Yeah," I said, "Lucifer lied to you... that's what he does, that's why we call him the father of lies. I wish I could tell you that he was finished with you, but for you it's just beginning. For the rest of your lives he is going to torment you by reminding you of what you have lost."

Bella and I helped them up and into the house where we would begin the process of getting them settled on their new planet and into their new lives.

***

SECTION #16

Essay CONCLUSION:

Needless to say, we made it back safely and I think this is as good a place as any to conclude this assignment.

I'm not sure how much of this essay will actually be read by anyone. Most of what happened has been deemed classified, so I can't even discuss it let alone write about it in an assignment for school. The good news is, at least Russia and China were satisfied with my explanation. Once we had the complete Pardes vocabulary, we were able to translate the entire transmission. They are desperate now to reach Pardes.

(Yeah... that'll happen.)

The other good news, if you can call it good news, is that this case has helped me find a big missing piece to the puzzle that is my life. And now I know the truth. My father as well as Bella's were from Pardes. He was one of those who ate the forbidden fruit and was banished to Earth.

Yesterday I saved a world and I ran into four people who made the biggest mistake of their lives. At first

I wanted to tell them how stupid they were, but the truth is they were deceived by the devil and who can judge them for that... not me.

(That whole glass house and rocks thing).

Now all I feel is sadness for a paradise lost... for all of us.

When summer finally arrives I know I won't be out frolicking in the sun like the other kids. I explained it all to my mother and she cried but, she understood. Bella and I will be away for a while. We are going to Salvation Mountain to find our dads and we aren't coming back until we get some answers.

Chapter 28

ONE WEEK AFTER the travelers left for Earth, Aaron stood on the floor of the Great Hall before the judges of the Supreme Council. The four spheres appeared in front of him, right on schedule. The lights shown bright red, so bright that Aaron and the assembled judges had to shield their eyes. Then the red lights slowly moved to the front of each sphere and began arranging themselves into a recognizable message.

"DON'T EAT," pulsed on each sphere in an almost ominous warning.

"DON'T COME," next appeared.

The auditors moved forward and verified that the spheres were authentic. Then as the link was severed, the spheres dropped to the ground and went dark forever.

Aaron stepped forward and looked down at the spheres; gone were their polished metallic sheen. Their once smooth exterior was replaced by pock marks, rust and decay from exposure to a fallen planet's atmosphere. Aaron marveled at the extent of the damage that occurred in such a short period of time.

A hazardous waste team moved in to secure and quarantine the contaminated spheres.

The Council's vote was unanimous.

"I think we can consider this matter resolved," Aaron said, addressing the Supreme Council.

An angry and defeated Lucifer watched and fumed. He had spent the last week trying to convince the four travelers to send a different message. His logic, though twisted, was undeniable. If they sent the message to "EAT" and "COME" then Pardes would fall. And if Pardes fell, then they could all go home.

He slipped out of his seat and headed for an exit without a word and no one even noticed.

After a moment of prayer for the four travelers, the rejoicing began. It started off as a low rumble and burst forward into a loud roar heard all over the world.

***

Made in the USA
Charleston, SC
07 February 2012